*Adam Heard the Abrupt Crash
and the Shattering of Glass
Mixed with a Strange Animal Cry.*

He rushed to the living room. Blood was splattered in front of the fireplace. To the left of it lay a small white object.

For a moment Adam thought it was a baby.

Slowly, he walked toward it, studied it before picking it up gently.

A kitten. A dead kitten. Not more than a day or two old.

Then he saw the tiny piece of paper folded over and over, tied to a string around the kitten's neck. He pulled it loose and managed to unfold it with his free hand.

The message was simple, stark:

"More of a shot than Robert got."

Richard Breen

ADAM'S CHILD

A modern horror story

A Dell Original
Dell/Seymour Lawrence

A Dell/Seymour Lawrence Book
Published by
Dell Publishing Co., Inc.
1 Dag Hammarskjold Plaza
New York, New York 10017

Dell ® TM 681510, Dell Publishing Co., Inc.

ISBN: 0-440-10917-5

Printed in the United States of America

First printing—October 1978

Il n'y a pas de morts.
(There are no dead.)

Maurice Maeterlinck.

CHAPTER 1

His name is Adam Reynolds. He is forty-three years old, and until three months ago his life was what you might call "quietly normal" for a middle-aged bachelor. He went to the movies occasionally, dated occasionally, drank a little too much occasionally.

He is a big man, this Adam Reynolds: six feet five inches; 247 pounds, with a farm-boy thickness to his shoulders and forearms and waist—a bulkiness that gives his torso the appearance of being too substantial for his long, thin legs to support. It is the kind of body professional athletes walk around in, years after their days of discipline and glory have vanished; a blending of bone and flesh and metabolism that consistently defeats any diet designed to bring its wearer's weight in line with what the insurance companies would like. It is the body, as Adam Reynolds's doctor is apt to repeat three times a year, of a classic cardiac arrest waiting for its chance of a lifetime.

"If you don't take care of your heart, Adam, one of these days your heart is going to take care of you. Cut down on the calories and cholesterol. And the liquor. And if you can't quit smoking completely, see that you cut down as much as humanly possible. I'm not only saying this as your doctor, Adam, I'm saying it as your doubles partner."

And so, once a month, or at the very least, once every two months, Adam Reynolds made a secret and solemn vow to get rid of the extra thirty-five pounds which were making his heart pump harder than it should have to, twenty-four hours a day, seven days a week, fifty-two weeks a year.

Adam Reynolds also promised to play tennis a little more often; not just doubles, but singles, too. He promised to ride his bicycle religiously. And knock off the after-work martinis. And to stop smoking completely. But Adam never kept the promises for much longer than a week or two, because, like so many people journeying from their forties to their fifties, Adam Reynolds was acutely aware that he wasn't going to be watching the eleven o'clock news and *The Late Show* forever. And if he couldn't at least enjoy a drink or a cigarette with his coffee or a baked potato bathed in butter, then he'd just as soon vacate the premises—and let someone say the words over him right now. In fact, Adam Reynolds had reached the point where he seldom lifted a martini to his lips without offering a quiet toast.

"Nobody lives forever," he would say before taking that first, quick little sip from the rim of his glass. The toast not only made the martini taste better, it made Adam Reynolds feel that drinking was a good and sensible, and yes, even a noble thing to do.

And there were times when Adam Reynolds needed very much to feel good and sensible and noble, because, at times, Adam's job as creative director for Martin-Philbrick, Inc., the third largest advertising agency in South Florida, could twist his forty-three-year-old nerves into tight little knots that caused just the slightest tremor of a hand, the almost imperceptible twitch of an eyelid.

But Adam liked his job. Perhaps liked isn't exactly the right word. At least he was never really bored or unhappy with his job. There was always the day-to-day tension of deadlines and client presentations and rumors of accounts to be gained or lost. There was a stimulation to the job, a sense of responsibility to the artists and copywriters on his creative team, an edgy desire to do advertising that didn't insult the public's intelligence, and yet, as Mr. Philbrick would often say at the office, "would ring the cash register for the client."

Probably the best thing about Adam's job—from Adam's point of view—was that he was never chained to his desk from nine to five. He was fairly free to make his own schedule. Arrive at the office late, but within reason. Leave early, but within reason. Take long lunch hours, but within reason. If one had a reputation as a good creative director at Martin-Philbrick, Inc., one enjoyed certain privileges.

One of the privileges that Adam enjoyed most was leaving the office and disappearing into a movie theater or a library or a department store whenever the rainy season reached him too deeply: when he'd look out his office window and suddenly couldn't remember a day when it hadn't been raining.

When there is a particularly long and heavy rainy season in South Florida, it can have dramatic effects on certain people. A long rainy season, like the one just finished, gave Adam Reynolds a feeling of almost constant melancholy coupled with extreme lethargy which made getting out of bed in the morning seem like an achievement of almost epic proportions. Adam Reynolds felt as if someone had sealed the skies shut with a steel zipper, forcing the awesome weight of the atmosphere down on his mind and body. The constant humidity clogged his sinuses. His fingers and toes, already fleshy, became puffed. They ached continuously, but especially in the early part of the day, and again late at night. The grass around Adam Reynolds's house grew thick and soggy and seemed to turn into green slime sucking at his shoes as he moved across the lawn each morning to pick up the *Miami Herald,* which was invariably flooded inside a plastic bag. The branches of trees swelled and sagged. Huge puddles caused the regular parade of rush-hour traffic passing his house to slow to a funereal pace, headlights mournfully beaming through the late-afternoon haze or hard downpour. And then, at night, when the rain had finally stopped, Adam would listen for the frogs in his backyard. First one would croak. Then another. Then a thousand.

Adam Reynolds's house feels the rain. It is a big, old three-story Spanish house. It was built in 1927, so it's really not all that old. But in South Florida, anything built before 1950 is considered antique.

The house gives the appearance of a fortress, or so Adam Reynolds's neighbors have told him. And, on a rainy day, with the drapes drawn and the large jalousie windows rolled tight, the appearance of a deserted fortress. It dominates the street it is located on in Coral Gables. All of the other six houses on the street are one story. Four were built in the 1940s. One in the 1960s. And one was completed last year.

It gave Adam Reynolds a nice feeling to know that for a long time his house was the only house on the street. It must have been quite grand back in the twenties and thirties, he often thought. Even now, it is still one of the handsomest houses in Coral Gables. It has dignity. It has character. But Adam Reynolds's house was meant for sunshine. It suffers during the rainy season. Just as Adam Reynolds suffers.

Adam realized the house was impractical for him. Much too big for one man living alone. And yet, he loved its bigness. He loved the enormous wrought-iron chandelier that hung majestically from the foyer ceiling, its fourteen candlelike lights creating the impression of an elegant birthday cake suspended in space.

He loved the Cuban tile floors with their intricate patterns that changed from flowers to faces to stars depending on which angle he was viewing them from. Then there were the long, narrow bookshelves that lined the living-room wall, serving as a resting place not only for volumes on philosophy and theater, but also for a mahogany bust of Cervantes and a tintype of Adam Reynolds's great-grandmother, and assorted rocks and clocks and lanterns and ashtrays and other relics of his trips to South America and Europe.

Adam Reynolds loved the arched entrance to each room and the absence of doors between rooms—except for the massive Florida pine front door with its ponderous brass knocker. But most of all, he loved the feeling of history in the house. The awareness that other people had lived in the house before him, and that other people would live in the house after he'd gone. The house had been his companion. It gave him a feeling of permanence, of continuity: a feeling he could never hope to find in newer houses or apartments.

But really, the house was much too big for Adam Reynolds, especially since he'd lost interest in entertaining at home over the last few years. He could not sleep in the six bedrooms at the same time. He had no need for five bathrooms. And he could not keep up with the constant repairs the house required. He had held onto the house all these years because its value had kept increasing at an exceptional rate. Virtually all property in Coral Gables had grown dramatically in value during the fifties and sixties, but large, old, three-story Spanish houses like his were obviously commodities not easily duplicated or replaced. And so while the value of other houses in the area had increased considerably, the value of Adam Reynolds's house had soared. It was, in effect, his one and only source of accumulated wealth, his nest egg for retirement. But it was quite impractical for a bachelor.

"One day soon," he often said to friends, "I shall probably sell it and find something smaller, something more practical." When he did, though, he knew he would miss it terribly. After all, it had been his home for twenty-one years.

Twenty-one years? Had it really been that long since he and Louise first opened the front door? Adam often recalled the fine, flowing red hair and the porcelain skin and the large blue eyes that locked a well of loneliness inside them.

Late at night, when consciousness began to crumble into sleep, Adam Reynolds could hear Louise talking to him across the years. "Why am I so afraid, Adam? Why do I wake up at night and know that something horrible is going to happen to us?" The blue-moon eyes would disappear behind the fluttering white clouds of her eyelids.

"Don't be silly, sweetheart," Adam could hear his own voice say, "nothing terrible is going to happen to us. We're young and healthy. And besides, I have to get up for work tomorrow morning at seven."

Louise had been right, of course. Something horrible did happen to them. But that was a long time ago and Adam Reynolds rarely thought about it now, except in that brief period at night before his mind surrendered to sleep. What bothered Adam more than the tragedy of his past was the way he could now feel life constantly reminding him of his own mortality, through his own aching fingers and the cluster of varicose veins that bulged around his right ankle, and the irritating little sore that kept reappearing on his chest.

"Forty-three," he would tell himself a few times a week while driving to work, "forty-three isn't really very old."

And then, driving home from work, he would see things differently. "Forty-three," Adam would say, "isn't very young."

Little changes had begun to take place in Adam's life. He had begun to read the obituary column in the *Miami Herald;* not every day, but often enough to be aware that death comes more suddenly and more frequently to people in their forties than to people in their thirties.

Adam had also begun to read his own face and he did not enjoy the story he found there. It was a tired face. Not dramatically tired. Not nobly tired. Just tired.

The gray-green eyes that used to laugh and shine at every chance had now become almost permanently quiet and ordinary. His face had more lines than it had had a few years before, especially around the eyes. That was to be expected. But instead of adding character to his features, the lines merely added age. The hair was almost completely gray now. So were the eyebrows.

Adam Reynolds was going to die. Not necessarily any day soon. But he was going to die. One day he would just no longer be. No more Adam. No more Reynolds. No more 247 pounds. Adam had always known that everyone dies. Three of his dogs had died while he was growing up, and little Adam Reynolds himself had buried two of them. Friends had died as early as the third grade. Richie Evers who always had black-and-blue marks on his arms and legs, and nosebleeds that never seemed to stop, started coughing up blood one day on the bus coming home from school. Some of the blood got on Adam Reynolds's shirt. Adam's mother couldn't wash it out. Richie Evers didn't come to school the next day. Mrs. Evers wanted Adam to have Richie's bicycle and roller skates and the football pants that had been worn only once. Adam's mother made him say no.

Relatives had died, as recently as six months ago. Adam's cousin Marguerite, a woman who was always quiet, composed, and perhaps a bit too eager to please, waited until her three children had gone off to school one morning, making sure that each one had received a big happy kiss as they raced out the front door. Then she walked upstairs, put a revolver in her mouth, and pulled the trigger. The youngest child, Eric, was the first one home from school. He made a peanut butter and jelly sandwich and walked upstairs to tell his mother that he and Barry Peters were going to have the biggest parts in the class play.

Adam Reynolds had always known that someday he, too, would die. But during this past rainy season it was different. He *knew*. He really *knew*. And that made it a bit more difficult to get up every morning to go to work at Martin-Philbrick, Inc. And a bit more difficult to come home every evening to a large, empty house. And in between, a bit more difficult to concentrate on creating advertising campaigns and to carry on conversations and remember to do things like pick up his clothes at the dry cleaners and take his tape recorder in for repair and go about the everyday business of living.

And so, since the future held nothing but the arrival of nothingness, Adam Reynolds made increasingly frequent trips back to the days when the gray-green eyes laughed and shone. Back to the days when he ordered his first martini, sold his first ad campaign. It was safer territory back there. Cancer didn't exist back there. Nor did emphysema. Nor collisions on the Palmetto Expressway. Nor heart attacks. Certainty existed back there. You knew where you were going. You knew what was going to happen. And you knew one thing for sure. You knew you weren't going to die back there. Adam Reynolds knew that there were only two places in the entire world where he could die. The present. And the future. And so he avoided them as much as possible. And he kept on making a toast whenever he lifted a drink to his lips. "Nobody lives forever," he would say. And then he'd wink.

One night last year—it was a rainy Thursday about eleven fifteen—Adam Reynolds was sitting alone in his living room watching Spencer Tracy send pilots over Tokyo and change the course of history.

Adam had seen the movie before, many years before, when everybody knew Americans were the good guys and that dropping bombs from behind the cover of clouds was unquestionably an act of heroism. Now, the film seemed grotesquely dated. But Adam was enjoying it. He enjoyed anything with Tracy.

Adam reached for the can of Budweiser that rested on the black-and-red ottoman at his side and wondered how long it had been since he'd first seen the film. Twenty-five years, he'd bet. Twenty-five years ago. A lifetime ago, a whole different country ago. Adam drained the last drops from the Budweiser can and made a mental note not to get himself wrapped up in all that "the way the country has changed" business that had been the tired topic of conversation at virtually every cocktail party he'd been to in the past several years.

Forget it, he thought. Everything changes. So America's changed. So my cholesterol count has changed. So people live and breathe and eat and sing and make love and grow old and die. So big deal. Nobody lives forever.

The TV screen filled with the craggy features of Tracy as he briefed his men on the most important mission they'd ever fly.

I'll bet they synchronize their watches, thought Adam.

The phone rang. Adam got up from the large leather and wood Spanish chair he'd been sitting in and walked through an arched doorway, down a long foyer, and stopped at the alcove that housed an old rolltop desk, and just above the desk on the wall, a white phone. Adam squeezed, then dropped the empty can of Budweiser into a wastebasket beside the desk. The phone rang for perhaps the sixth or seventh time. Adam picked up the receiver and plopped down into a swivel chair that sat directly in front of the desk.

"Hello," said Adam absently, his mind still wondering whether or not the fliers were synchronizing their watches. There was no answer.

"Hello," repeated Adam. He began to wonder who would be calling him at home this late on a week night. Silence on the other end of the line.

"Hey," said Adam, "who is this? Speak up or I'm going to hang up." Still no answer. Adam was about to place the receiver back in its cradle when he thought he heard a faint sound break the silence for a second. The sound had barely been audible, and Adam couldn't tell if it was a soft sigh, a quick breath, or simply his imagination. He listened more intently. Nothing but silence for perhaps ten seconds. Quietly, Adam hung up the phone and returned to the living room to see what was happening to World War II.

No sooner had Adam settled into the large and comfortable Spanish chair than the phone started ringing again. This time the rings seemed louder, more irritating. "Damn," said Adam as he pushed himself up from the chair and headed for the alcove. He picked up the phone and was just about to speak when he heard that same soft sound he thought he had heard only a moment before. What was it? And then Adam had the answer because he could clearly recognize the sounds that followed as the nonsensical gurgling of a baby. He listened in great fascination for a moment, wondering how a baby, obviously a very young baby, could be operating a telephone. Before Adam could formulate the next question in his own mind, he heard an awkward clanging sound as if the receiver on the other end of the line had been dropped. Then there was a sudden click and the steady hum of a dial tone.

Adam stood silently in the alcove. He placed the receiver in its cradle and turned to walk back to the living room. When he reached the foyer, he stopped and stared at his own shadow looming large against the wall. Adam could understand a baby playing with a phone and dialing his number by pure chance. Things like that happened all the time. But how could a baby playing with a phone dial his number correctly twice within the space

of a minute or two? That was totally impossible.
The whole thing was just a weird coincidence.

And then the phone rang again. Adam turned
and walked back to the alcove. He picked up the
receiver, placed it next to his ear, and then pulled
it back quickly because the sound was shrill and
piercing to his ear. It continued, high-pitched and
grating, and it took Adam Reynolds a few seconds
to realize that he was listening to a baby crying.

Adam's first instinct was to hang up. He didn't.
"Is anyone there?" he asked.

The baby screamed louder.

"Hey," Adam spoke harshly into the phone
now, "is anybody there? What's going on?"

The cries grew louder, stronger, more agitated.
It was the kind of incessant, desperate screaming
that drives young mothers to nervous breakdowns
and even to acts of brutality. Adam tried to sort
his own thoughts, to determine what was actually happening, but the baby's screaming kept
him from thinking clearly.

The cries grew even more intense, more painful,
and that's when Adam recognized something in
the baby's screams that frightened him. It wasn't
just a baby crying, he realized, it was an infant.
Perhaps a newborn infant.

The same imagination that made Adam an ef-
fective creative director now worked against him.
Seated in the swivel chair, listening to an infant
screaming over the phone, he started to trace the
call in his mind's eye.

He could see a woman, a young woman, stand-

ing beside a crib. In the crib was an infant, its face
red, its fists closed, its fingernails so small as to be
barely visible. The woman was pale and gaunt.
She moved toward the phone slowly, with great
discomfort and apparent weakness in her step.
The phone rested on a small night table beside the
crib. The woman picked up the receiver. She
dialed a number, then placed a hand over the
speaker and waited for someone to answer the
phone. When someone answered, she placed the
phone inside the crib next to the infant's face.
Then she removed her hand from the speaker,
bent, and kissed the infant on the cheek. She
straightened up, turned, and quickly left the
room, closing the door behind her, leaving the infant completely alone except for whoever was listening on the other end of the phone.

For just a second or two Adam thought he
might be the baby's only link with the world.
Then, to put the bizarre episode back in perspec-
tive, the baby on the other end of the phone suddenly stopped crying. After a moment or two it
actually started making soft, warm sounds as if it
were getting a bottle or all the attention it needed.
Then there was a click at the other end of the line
and the sudden, monotonous hum of a dial tone.

Adam rose from the chair and stood in the alcove, staring absently at the receiver in his hand.
Then he placed it back in its cradle. As he walked
toward the living room and Spencer Tracy, Adam
wondered who could possibly have made such
strange calls.

How could a baby that young—an infant—have cried directly into the phone unless someone held the speaker next to the child's mouth? Who would do such a thing? And for what reason? A practical joke? No. It had obviously been a wrong number. But three wrong numbers? Adam didn't want to let himself think there was an abandoned baby somewhere crying for help. But the baby couldn't have been alone. After all, how could a baby who sounded so young even hold a phone? For that matter, how could the baby hang it up? No, thought Adam, it was just one of those strange things that happen in life. It would be silly even to speculate as to how and why a child was screaming at him over the phone that late at night.

Adam sat down in the large wood and leather Spanish chair in the living room. A commercial for a men's clothing store was temporarily interrupting World War II. It was a commercial that Adam had conceived at Martin-Philbrick, Inc. The idea, he thought, had been good. The execution of the idea, he realized now, was terrible. He watched the client's name fade out over the logo and felt that curious sense of shame he always felt when an ad or commercial he had worked on turned out badly. He knew he would take a ribbing from his competitors and he knew that a few more commercials like that and his reputation as one of the best creative directors in South Florida would be severely damaged. For the next hour, as he watched Tokyo burst into flames, Adam Reynolds could not get his mind off how badly the commercial for the men's clothing store had played on television. The interruption—the phone call with the screaming infant at the end of the line—had been completely forgotten.

Later, lying in bed mere seconds away from sleep, Adam could sense another presence in the room. It was Louise. He could see her face, her fine, flowing red hair. Her lips moved, but no words came from them. Instead, there was a painful sound that Adam had heard earlier. It was the sound of a baby crying. A young baby. An infant.

Then there was the sound of a phone receiver clicking and the steady drone of a dial tone.

Louise disappeared.

Adam slipped off to sleep.

He dreamed of his mother.

CHAPTER 2

The night following the incident of the phone call, Adam Reynolds spent the evening with Dom Petrella, the director of Bay Hill for Boys, a nondenominational institution for boys without parents, and for boys whose social problems had become too severe for their parents to handle.

The two middle-aged men had virtually grown up together, and even though their professional careers had taken them on disparate courses, Adam and Dom had remained very close friends, seeing each other frequently, sharing with each other insights into their two quite different worlds: the often illusory world of advertising and the sometimes too realistic world of social work.

This particular evening—a rainy evening—they had returned to Adam's home for some drinks and conversation after watching the Bay Hill basketball team lose to a squad of local teenagers by the score of 78 to 46.

They were seated in the living room in front of the artificial fireplace that was framed in swirling, wrought-iron arches. Just above the fireplace, inscribed in tile on the black-and-white marble mantelpiece, were ancient Arabic words which a scholar guest had once translated, "The only reliance is in God." Directly in front of the fireplace a large, round mahogany table—chipped and worn and weathered by years of damp tropical air—served as the resting place for a bottle of Dewar's Scotch, a bronze ice bucket flecked with rust, and two substantial drinking glasses. Above the table, a red-and-green Tiffany lamp hung from the twelve-foot ceiling on a thin golden chain, a crystal Christmas wreath suspended in space, with a soft white globe peeking out like the silver underbelly of a lonely moon.

Adam fixed Scotch on the rocks for both of them, noticing as he poured that his fingers had again grown puffy and stiff in the warm, moist night air. He reminded himself to take three aspirin before going to bed.

Dom's broad, ruddy face flinched into a tight little grimace that revealed an upper tooth lined with gold. Dom spoke. "Those kids of mine are something, aren't they?" As if to agree, a chorus of frogs began croaking in the wet blackness of Adam Reynolds's backyard.

Adam reached across the large mahogany table, handed Dom one of the two Scotches, and quickly raised the remaining glass in a silent toast. Dom nodded, lifted his glass, then both men completed the ritual they so frequently shared by downing their first drink of the evening in one smooth and seemingly coordinated motion. Adam immediately began to pour fresh drinks.

"Jesus Christ," snapped Dom, as if the sudden infusion of Scotch had awakened his anger, "all week in practice they look like UCLA and the Knicks combined, and then the night of the game they go out there and play like Groucho Marx. Tonight, though, they did something really new and different. Tonight, I think they invented the slow break."

Adam smiled absently and handed Dom his second drink of the evening, a much fuller glass than the first.

Adam brought his hands together, made a bridge of his fingers, and placed his nose atop the peak of the bridge. He spoke with the voice of authority and experience. "I know you're disappointed for the kids, but don't let it get you. It's a long season."

Dom ran his forefinger down the full length of a prominent Italian nose that made a sharp left turn before it dipped into a black Zapata mustache. "The way they played tonight, you're goddamned right it's going to be a long season."

"C'mon, Dom. How can you get so wrapped up in a kid's game? It's not the pros, you know. You just can't take it all that seriously."

Dom's lips pulled back tight over his teeth. "That's the goddamned problem. You see the parents and the girlfriends of the kids on the other team? They were serious about who was going to win. They cheered and screamed and carried on like they were watching Bill Walton play Kareem Abdul-Jabbar for a million dollars." Dom began to puff on a little cigar.

"You see our side of the floor?" He kept on puffing and talking. "You see who our kids had cheering for them? Cute little girlfriends with perky little asses? Not on your life. Proud parents and brothers and sisters? Guess again. You know who our kids had cheering for them? Me. That's who. Me. The half-bald old bastard who gets paid to keep them in line. The warden who tells them they can't go into town at night. The rat who gives them a hard time when they flunk math or show up with a case of clap. Me. The fink who knows all the dirty little secrets they want to keep hidden from the world and from each other and even from themselves. That's who's cheering for them. Me. And you. A Wop do-gooder and a fat adman. Some cheering section, eh?"

"There was nothing to cheer about. They played a lousy game. Maybe you're a lousy coach. Did you ever think about that?"

Dom stared down into the ice cubes. "Oh, Jesus, Adam. Sometimes I can't believe you're that goddamned dumb. Or insensitive."

Adam took a long drink of Scotch, then spoke in a tone he seldom used with Dom. "Look, Dr. Schweitzer. Or Father Flanagan. Or whoever you think you are. Please don't moralize to me. I'm not responsible for any of those kids. Sure, I feel bad that life has kicked them in the balls. But you want to know something? If you live long enough, life kicks everyone in the balls. Your kids lost a game. A goddamned ball game. Let's not beat it to death, okay?"

Dom was silent for a second, then spoke: "Okay, I'm sorry I'm so uptight. It's that little kid who played guard for us tonight."

"He in trouble?"

"They're all in trouble. But he's in real trouble. Up to his asshole. And I don't think I can pull him out."

Adam knew when Dom needed to ease something from his system, to release an ugly burden from inside his mind, as if by letting Adam know just how sick the world is, the world might somehow get better. Adam remained silent. He let Dom talk, and while Dom talked, Adam refilled their drinks.

"Harold came to us about six months ago. A weird little kid, I thought. Really quiet. Spooky quiet. I looked into his portfolio and I think I got a pretty good idea of why he was so quiet, so withdrawn."

Adam looked at his friend and wondered how Dom could possibly continue to care so much about children that were not his own. During the last year, Adam had found it increasingly difficult to care very much about anyone, about what happened to anyone, even Dom, even himself.

Dom continued: "Three years ago when Harold was twelve, his father came home one night, took a knife out of the kitchen drawer—a big carving knife. He cut Harold's mother's throat wide open.

The kid just stood there and watched. Then Harold's father cut his own throat wide open. They both bled to death in front of Harold in a matter of seconds. Harold stayed in the room alone with them and his dog for two days. A neighbor found Harold sitting between them, holding his dog in his lap."

Adam looked at the deep-set, dark brown eyes of his friend and he saw the pain that lived there, and he turned away, embarrassed by the pain. He sipped his drink. "I don't see how you stay on that job."

Dom smiled weakly at Adam. "It doesn't tear me up as much as it used to. I realize now I can't save the world. I realize I probably can't even save one kid in ten."

Adam poured Dom another drink. The rain made a soft rat-a-tat sound on the tile roof. And the frogs made the same deep-throated sounds their ancestors made thousands of years before the night Adam and Dom sat in the living room and talked about Harold's problems.

Dom spoke again: "Hell, it's not Harold's background that's bothering me. Half the kids out there have case histories that read like horror stories. No, it's what happened to him last week."

Adam nodded, silently giving Dom permission to continue the story.

"You remember I said that Harold stayed two days with his dead parents and his dog? Well, the authorities took the dog away from Harold. They had it put to sleep."

Adam lit a Marlboro. Dom crushed his little cigar in the large copper ashtray that rested on the mahogany table.

"They didn't do it to be cruel. They had to find a place for Harold. Bay Hill and places like Bay Hill obviously have to have some strict rules and one of those rules is no personal pets, period. I think you can understand that. I mean we can't have fifty scroungy dogs running around with fifty screwed-up kids, now can we?"

Adam nodded.

"Well, anyway, about four or five weeks ago, Harold and two or three of the other kids were out goofing off in the woods near our place and they came upon this sick old dog that was about ready to die. The other kids picked up rocks and were all set to use the old mutt for target practice. But Harold screamed and acted crazy and the other guys got a little scared and dropped their rocks and left the dog alone. And after that, Harold would sneak off into the woods every afternoon with some food and sit with the dog for hours. And when the dog was well enough to move, he smuggled it into his dormitory at Bay Hill."

The deep-set, dark Italian eyes were looking straight at Adam. Dom nervously lit another cigar. "You want me to go on? Am I boring you with this bullshit?"

Adam indicated with a gesture of his hand that he wished Dom to continue.

"Naturally, it wasn't long before I found out about the dog. And what a dog. Really mangy.

Only three legs. Worms. Fleas. You name it, this dog had it."

Adam heard a car, perhaps moving a little too quickly, turn onto Arica Circle.

"Anyway," said Dom, the slight shadow of a smile flickering across his face, "it was obvious to me that Harold was really hooked on this old dog and I think it's pretty easy to understand why. I just didn't have the heart to take it away from him. I made an exception. And I try not to make exceptions too often."

Adam nodded toward Dom's glass. "Ready?"

"No, not quite," said Dom, not realizing that his glass was now empty. "I told Harold that he could keep his dog. Not in the dormitory, of course. I told him he could build a doghouse. And that's what Harold did, and I'm telling you, the change in the kid was terrific. He watched over that old dog like a mother hen. It was quite a sight, 'Harold and his three-legged hound.' That's what the other kids called them."

Adam had known from the moment Dom started the story about Harold and his three-legged dog that it would have an unhappy ending. "Don't tell me the other kids did something to the dog?" he asked.

"No, no," said Dom, "but I'm sure a few of them would have liked to." He held out his glass to Adam, who poured with a heavy hand. "No," continued Dom, "it happened in the most crazy way you could imagine." He sipped his fresh drink.

"Most of the times when they went walking, Harold kept the dog on a leash. Not that the dog needed to be kept on a leash. I think it was simply Harold's way of showing that the dog belonged to him. Or that he belonged to the dog."

Adam sat silent, listening to Dom's words, but not certain he wanted to hear them.

"One day last week," Dom continued, "or maybe ten days ago, Harold took the dog for a walk down by our stables. You've seen our stables, haven't you?"

Adam nodded and took a long, slow drag on his cigarette.

"When he got there, he remembered that he'd left the sugar he'd saved for the horses in his dormitory. So he tied Dondi—that was the dog's name—he tied Dondi's leash to a board by the window in the stable. Then he ran back to his dorm to fetch the sugar. Apparently while Harold was gone, the old dog either got scared of the horses or simply wanted to follow Harold back to the dorm. Anyway, Dondi managed to climb up to the window ledge—which must have taken some effort on those three old legs—and jumped out of the window to follow Harold. Of course, the dog didn't realize the leash was still around its neck. The dumb dog hung himself."

Adam looked down into the amber liquid in his glass and blew little puffs of smoke into it.

Dom, too, looked into his glass of Scotch, as if he could see the events he had just described taking place there. Then he looked at Adam. "But that isn't the sick part."

Adam was beginning to get annoyed with Dom. The story was upsetting. Adam didn't like it. He didn't like to dwell on other people's problems, especially when he couldn't solve those problems, and especially when he had no desire to get caught up in those problems. After all, ugly, painful things happened to kids all over the world every single day of the week. Hadn't three of Adam's dogs died when he was a kid? He really didn't care to hear anymore, but there was something he wanted to find out, so he let Dom continue.

"The sick part," said Dom, reaching into the breast pocket of his polo shirt for a fresh little cigar, "the really sick part happened after the dog died. After Harold found it."

Dom lit the little cigar, exhaled smoke in a painful sigh, and went on with the story. "Harold just wouldn't or just couldn't accept the fact that the dog was dead. He carried the dog home from the stable in his arms. He put it back in its doghouse. He brought it food. He talked to it. He sang to it. And the damn dead dog just lay there like it was sleeping. Finally, after a few days, I got through to Harold. He seemed to accept the fact that the dog was dead. In fact, he insisted that he be the only one allowed to bury it. By that time you could smell the stench a couple of acres away."

Adam raised his glass. "Interesting story, Dom.

Do you know any more like that with such happy endings?"

Dom looked at Adam blankly. "The story isn't quite over. You see, the next day Harold came into my office and told me he would like to show me Dondi's grave. I agreed. And I told Harold that I thought he had shown courage and an acceptance of responsibility in choosing to bury Dondi himself."

Dom paused and again looked deep into his Scotch. The rhythm of the rain on the roof had grown more intense. The frogs croaked less frequently now, but with greater force than they had only a few moments earlier.

"We walked down to a spot near the stables, to the spot Harold had selected for Dondi's grave. It was right outside the stable window that Dondi had jumped through. The dog was buried all right. Or maybe I should say almost buried. Harold had covered all of Dondi with dirt, except for the dog's head. It was probably the sickest thing I've ever seen. A dead dog's head sticking straight up out of the ground. With flies buzzing all around it."

"Oh, Jesus, Jesus," moaned Adam, screwing up his face in an obvious look of distaste.

"The sick part of it," said Dom, "is that Harold didn't seem upset by it. He had candles lit all around the poor dog's decaying head. He didn't see anything wrong with it. He seemed proud. He asked me to pray for the dog's soul."

Dom's last statement was followed by a period

of strained silence, each of the men exploring his own private thoughts. Dom gazed down at the intricate patterns on the Cuban tile floor. Adam stared intently at Dom. The dark, deep-set eyes were weary, the lines surrounding them had multiplied considerably during the past two years. They further accented the fact that everything about Dom's head and facial features was oversized. His mouth was large, his nose larger, his ears larger still. And yet it was a pleasant, not unattractive face. It was strange to think of Dom as tired and worn down because physically he appeared enormously powerful. The strong-looking skull seemed to be growing through black-gray patches of Brillo. He stood slightly under six feet, but his frame was massive and muscular. It gave Dom a physical presence that could, and often did, dominate a room. Adam remembered laughing aloud when a mutual friend described Dom as "looking like two middle linebackers joined at the hip." It was an astonishingly accurate description. But Adam didn't feel like laughing now. He was concerned for his friend. But he was far more concerned for himself.

"Dom," Adam broke the silence, "maybe I've got no business bringing this up now, but I think I'd be a fool not to in light of what you've told me about Harold's background."

Dom brought his gaze back from the Cuban tile floor to meet Adam's eyes. "What are you talking about?"

"Harold," answered Adam. "I believe Harold is

a very sick and very dangerous young person. I think we can all understand why he's screwed up. But that doesn't change the fact that he could be very dangerous right now."

Dom picked up his Scotch. He glared at Adam. "You think you know something about Harold that I don't? As far as I know, tonight was the first time you've ever seen him."

Adam rose from the black leather sofa, his face suddenly hidden from Dom's view by the large red-and-green Tiffany lamp that hung directly over the table. From Dom's point of view, he could only see Adam from his knees to his neck. Adam's voice came from behind the globe of the Tiffany.

"When Harold came out of the game tonight, he walked right past me. You were down at the other end of the bench so you couldn't see us. As he walked past me, Harold stopped for a second and looked straight into my eyes. I have never seen such naked hatred in my life. He spoke to me, very slowly, very directly. There could be no mistake about it: he was speaking to me. He looked at me and he said the words 'Mother Fucker.' He said them twice. And both times he said them, he clearly said them as two separate words. Not 'Motherfucker.' But 'Mother Fucker.' He paused between the words for effect. He said it twice. And then he said, 'You Mother Fuckers are gonna get yours. And you're gonna get it soon.' I wasn't going to mention it. But now, after what you've told me about him . . ."

Adam sat down on the sofa. Oddly, Dom didn't seem shaken by Adam's comments. "You scared?" Dom asked. "You scared of a fifteen-year-old kid?"

Adam thought for a long moment. He sipped his Scotch. He put his head back and stared up at the ceiling. He could see a damp, dark circle where rain was starting to seep through. "I don't know. I don't see what harm he could possibly do me. And yet, I guess I'm not too happy about the whole episode, especially after what you told me. But scared? I really don't know."

Dom spoke softly: "You should be scared. Every now and then I come across a kid I think is capable of anything. I think Harold's in that category."

"Then why keep him around Bay Hill where he can cause a lot of trouble and contaminate other kids?"

Dom held out his glass to Adam for a refill. "You heard the kid's background. Jesus Christ, for someone coming from something like that, the kid's an absolute angel. And besides, he hasn't done anything wrong yet. Crazy, maybe. But nothing really wrong. Except for threatening you. And hell, if they put people away for calling you a motherfucker, half of Dade County would be in jail tonight."

The tension in the room eased a little. Adam smiled. Dom did the same. They decided to have more drinks. It was going to be one of those nights: an all nighter, a long-drawn-out evening of drinking and discussion and arguments. After

Dom made the point that Harold had always tested out reasonably well with the staff psychologist, the conversation gradually drifted in other directions, and as is often the case when close friends share vast quantities of Scotch, subjects that had remained locked away for years slipped out of their hiding places to seek sympathy, and perhaps understanding.

At some point, a number of drinks later, Dom mentioned that he was thinking about hiring a female social psychologist on a part-time basis to help him at Bay Hill.

"She's got the credentials," he said, "but I'm a little concerned about her lack of experience and her age. She's only twenty-two."

An empty smile creased Adam's face. "Funny," he said, "I still think of Louise as being twenty-two."

"I didn't know you still thought about Louise." Dom poured Dewar's over the slivers of ice remaining in his glass. "I don't think I've heard you even mention Louise the last ten or twelve years."

The sound of rain on the roof underscored the silence in the room.

"Oh, yes," Adam answered dryly, "I still think of Louise."

Dom sipped his Scotch, then spoke: "You've never really opened up to me about her, you know. And I've never asked you to because I always figured you had your own reasons for not wanting to talk about her. I never wanted to pry into something that's painful for you. And I don't want to start prying now just because we're both up to our assholes in Scotch."

Again, that strange, forced smile crossed Adam's face. "No, you're not prying, Dom. And I don't feel pain. I haven't felt any pain about Louise in years." He paused, puffed on his cigarette, the ashes threatening to spill onto his lap. "You never knew Louise, did you?"

"Of course, I knew her. Who do you think was best man at your wedding? I remember, I even caught the bride's garter. And here I am, more than twenty years later, still a goddamned bachelor."

The ashes spilled, unnoticed, onto Adam's lap. "No, that's not what I meant," said Adam, the Scotch now making his tongue thick. "Of course, you knew her. I remember that. But you never really knew her, knew what kind of a person she was."

Dom rubbed the bridge of his nose with a stubby, hairy finger. "I really don't know how to answer that, Adam. It's been so long. But I guess nobody really knew Louise very well. Nobody but you. All I can remember was that she was very beautiful. And that there was something terribly fragile about her. Something that communicated a kind of defenselessness. Like she was born to be hurt. Not in a masochistic way, just in a way that made people worry about her. I've seen a few other people with that look. Like they're born to suffer. And the sad part is, they seem to know it."

Adam drained his Scotch.

Dom's deep brown eyes looked directly at Adam. "I wasn't the only one. I remember what my mother said to me the day of your wedding. She said, 'That's a lovely girl Adam's marrying. But there's something so sad about her. It's as if she knows she's not going to live very long.'"

"Well," said Adam, getting up to fix himself another Scotch, "Louise certainly fooled your mother. She's still alive and your mother's been dead for years. And I wouldn't be surprised if Louise outlives us all."

"You call that living?" said Dom, his voice heavy with too much Scotch. Dom sat looking at his friend. Neither one of the men spoke or moved. Then, after what must have been a full minute of silence, Adam said he wanted to tell Dom a story he had never told anyone. He said that he would try to tell it clearly and honestly, but so much time had passed and so many memories had been twisted or blurred that he could not be sure that the story he would tell Dom that night was the absolute truth. But it was going to be an attempt at the truth. It was the story of Louise. And what happened to her.

CHAPTER 3

It took Adam the better part of an hour and three heavy Scotches to tell Dom exactly what had happened to Louise. "There's more to tell," he said finally, "but it's getting late and maybe we'd better knock off for now while we can still see each other, and while I can still stand up."

Adam started to rise from his chair.

The lights went out. Quickly. Quietly. Without even a flickering warning. For a second or two, the room seemed to exist without dimension; there was only total blackness and nervous silence. Adam blinked rapidly, his eyes scanning the blackness, seeking an object, an outline, a silhouette—anything he could use as a point of focus.

"Fucking Florida Power and Light does it again," he mumbled in mock despair.

"Don't drink the Scotch, you go blind," Dom bellowed into the darkness. Then he laughed, a soft, distinctive, and slightly sadistic sound, which, coupled with the darkness, gave Adam the feeling he had barged into someone else's nightmare.

Finally Adam's eyes could make out the shape of the Tiffany lamp. Then the mahogany bust of Cervantes. He thought he could make out the black sphere that was Dom's head.

"Can you see anything?"

"I can see you, I think."

"Got a match?"

"They're on the table."

"Where the hell is the table?"

"Right in front of you."

Four hands groped around in the darkness on the coffee table until one of the hands hit the bottle of Scotch and sent it rolling off the table and crashing to the floor.

"Aw, shit," whined Dom.

"All right, don't move," said Adam. "I think I can find a flashlight. There's one in the desk."

Adam rose slowly from his chair, and much like a GI moving through a minefield, he took a gingerly first step, then another, moving slowly until he was certain he was on safe footing.

"I've heard of people getting blind, fucking drunk," he half laughed over his shoulder, "but this is ridiculous."

There was silence for a second as he waited for Dom's response, but the only appreciation for his humor was voiced by the ever-present frogs. Their croaking grew louder, mingling with the steady rattling of the rain on the roof and in the backyard. Adam lurched slowly into the foyer. Barely visible ahead was the alcove which housed the desk where he was sure he would find the flashlight. Then the phone rang. The sound interrupted the heavy darkness of the foyer almost as if it were a blast of light. Adam moved quickly toward the phone.

As Adam felt for the receiver, he wondered through clouds of Scotch why anyone would call at this hour unless it had something to do with the power failure. He picked up the phone and placed the receiver next to his ear. He recognized the sounds coming from the receiver almost at once. It was baby talk, an occasional "Ah, goo" mixed in with "da da da" and "na nan na" and "ma mam ma."

Adam said nothing. He stood in the darkness, listening. Then the garbled baby talk stopped and the voice at the other end kept repeating one simple phrase over and over and over. "Da da da da da da." Adam started to speak, but the voice kept chattering, "Da da da da da." Adam suddenly felt frightened and angry and confused.

From out of the darkness, Dom's voice interrupted: "Hey, Adam, I'm going to hit the road." He was speaking to Adam across the intense blackness of the foyer. "No sense sitting around here half smashed in the dark when we have to get up in the morning. Besides, that was the end of the goddamned Scotch."

Adam could hear the front door open. He saw Dom's burly frame silhouetted against a streetlight and framed in the doorway. Dom walked unsteadily out into the night. Just before he closed the door, he turned and spoke to Adam, who was still standing in the alcove, phone to his ear, hand cupped over the receiver. "We'll talk about Louise some more on another night soon. You can tell me the whole story. When we have more Scotch. And I don't have to get up in the morning." The door closed, Dom disappeared, and Adam turned his full attention back to the playful sounds of the baby on the phone.

"Da da da da da," the baby crooned into the blackness of the alcove that enveloped Adam. His patience broke.

"What the hell is going on? I don't know who you are, or where you are, or why in God's name you're wasting your time calling here with this craziness, but I swear to Almighty Jesus, if I ever find out who you are, I'm gonna pull your asshole out through your mouth. Now goddamn it, leave me alone. It's four o'clock in the fucking morning." Adam paused. The voice on the other end of the line had stopped its chant. There were perhaps five seconds of silence. Then Adam heard the baby's voice again. "Bye-bye, Da da, bye-bye, Da da." Then a click and the monotonous hum of a dial tone. Adam placed the receiver back in its cradle on the wall. He felt weak, almost nauseous. Too much Scotch, he thought. There was an abrupt crash in the living room, the shattering sound of glass breaking, mixed with a strange animal cry.

"Dom, for chrissakes, are you all right?" Adam yelled before he remembered that Dom had already left.

Then Adam remembered why he'd come to the

desk in the first place. For the flashlight. He felt around for the front drawer on the left. There. That's it. He pulled it open with his right hand and began patting around inside the drawer with his left. There. He felt it. And the instant he did, the power suddenly went back on and the chandelier lights with the look of a birthday cake blazed brightly over Adam's head. Adam covered the forty or so feet between the foyer and the living room in a few long, quick strides. And then he saw it. There was a splattering of blood interrupting the precise patterns of the Cuban tiles in front of the fireplace. And just to the left of the splattered blood lay a small, white, furry object.

For an instant, Adam thought it was a baby.

Adam walked slowly over to the small, white, furry object. He bent and studied it for a second, before picking it up gently.

It was a kitten. Dead. Not more than a day or two old.

Then Adam saw the tiny piece of paper folded over and over and over again and tied to a piece of string around the dead kitten's neck. He pulled the paper loose from the string with one hand and managed to unfold it with the same hand while the dead kitten seemed to be sleeping peacefully in the other. There was a short message on the paper, written in a handwriting that Adam thought for the briefest instant looked strangely familiar. The message was simple:

"More of a shot than Robert got."

Before Adam could read the note a second time,

there was another crash. This one was heavier, louder, and even more startling than the previous one. Glass flew past Adam's face. A small sliver nicked his forehead barely an inch above the eye. A trickle of blood oozed into his left eyebrow. Adam didn't notice. Instead he stared at the floor. A full-grown cat, its white fur flecked with blood, lay writhing in pain at his feet. It shrieked in agony, its back looking grotesquely broken into the shape of a question mark. Adam was sure it was going to die right in front of his eyes, in his living room, at four o'clock in the morning. He still cradled the dead kitten gently in one hand. He noticed that the kitten's white fur seemed identical to the white fur of the cat that lay in torment at his feet.

The cat shuddered and shrieked and clawed at the air, and then suddenly became very still and silent. She looked up at Adam with eyes that stared right through him.

"Aw, shit," he said aloud. "Shit, shit, shit."

CHAPTER 4

His name is Donald Schiff. He is thirty-nine years old, and the senior art director at Martin-Philbrick, Inc. Donald Schiff has an intense dislike for Adam Reynolds, not because Adam Reynolds is technically his professional superior, but because Donald Schiff has an intense dislike for practically everyone he has ever met. Or ever will meet.

He is one of those people, Donald Schiff, totally lacking in spontaneity or warmth, yet possessing an acid and sometimes amusing wit. He likes to think of himself as a contemporary Clifton Webb. Or perhaps a young George Sanders. His idea of an absolutely terrific time is seeing someone he knows—anyone he knows—embarrassed or uncomfortable.

There are always various whispers around the office concerning Donald Schiff's sex life. Sharon, the receptionist, swears he's a closet queen.

Joann, Mr. Philbrick's secretary, says that she heard from someone who knew Donald's ex-wife that he was either a transvestite, or impotent, or both. When asked what a transvestite was, Joann said that she thought it had something to do with making love to animals or dead people or something like that.

The prevailing view in the art department, however, was that Donald Schiff was into the leather boots and whips scene with either male or female partners, or assorted combinations thereof. At least that was the consensus for a while.

The truth is that no one knew very much about Donald Schiff and his sex life. Nonetheless it was obvious to practically everyone in the office that Donald Schiff wasn't normal the way everyone else in the office was normal. All anyone had to do was look at him. "It's written all over him, for chrissakes," said Bernie Stoneheim, the account executive, "he's a grade-A, bona fide, absolute fuckin' weirdo, with or without those goddamn Wedgies he wears. He comes into a room, you can actually feel the temperature drop. He stopped by my house to drop off some papers and my dog took one look at him and pissed all over the living-room floor. But I'll say one thing about the son of a bitch. He's a terrific art director. He knows his stuff. And he makes his deadlines. And he doesn't bust my clients' chops. And as long as he does that, I could give a shit less if he goes down every night on the entire starting offensive line of the Miami Dolphins."

It so happened that in the days immediately following the incident of the dead kitten and mangled cat, Adam Reynolds made the unfortunate

mistake of mentioning the bizarre episode to a few
people at Martin-Philbrick, Inc. Of course, word
eventually got around to Donald Schiff, who,
given such dramatic subject matter, knew how to
treat it accordingly.

"I hear a couple of cats dropped in on you un-
announced the other evening, Adam." The grin
that accompanied Donald Schiff's remarks could
only be described as an inspired leer. Without
waiting for Adam to acknowledge his comment or
even his presence, Donald Schiff lowered his
bony, five-foot-seven-inch frame onto the buffalo
hide sofa opposite Adam's desk. He glared at
Adam through thick steel-rimmed glasses that fit-
ted his personality so perfectly he might have
been born wearing them.

Adam looked up from his typewriter and stared
blankly at the pasty complexion of the intruder he
had once described as the Marquis de Sade of the
Pepsi Generation.

"Good morning, Donald. Did you want to see
me? I was so busy concentrating I didn't even
hear you knock."

Donald Schiff's leer shifted slowly into a smile
of admiration, communicating to Adam a sense of
respect for a rather tasteful put-down.

"Touché, Adam. I didn't knock. I forgot to, and
I apologize. The only thing worse than bad man-
ners is bad breath, and you have been guilty of
both in your time."

Adam shook his head slowly from side to side,

the gesture silently saying, You'll never change, will you, Donald?

Donald Schiff mimicked Adam, shaking his head silently as if to answer, And why the fuck should I?

It was strange how things worked out, thought Adam. Here's a guy I personally hired six years ago when everyone, myself included, said don't do it. He's a good designer. Talented. Disciplined. A fine art director. But he's not worth the headaches he'll cause you. And yet Donald Schiff had one quality which Adam Reynolds found irresistible. Donald Schiff was different. He was a different kind of person from anyone Adam had ever known. Destructive. Perhaps even dangerous—but surely more so to himself than anyone else? Neurotic as hell. But nonetheless a distinctive personality in a world Adam felt was increasingly populated by human beings spewn out of a Xerox machine.

Six years at Martin-Philbrick under Adam Reynolds's supervision had managed to mellow Donald Schiff a degree. He still strutted around the offices with an air of superiority that told everyone how painful it was for a gifted individual such as he to be forced into daily contact with such a collection of tasteless clods and Philistines. But at least now there was a bit of humor in his posturing. Initially he had carried his eccentricity like a painful burden. Now he flashed it like a prized possession.

The advent of middle age had not made Donald

Schiff a likable person or even an agreeable one to most of the people at Martin-Philbrick. It had merely made him tolerable.

In recent months, Adam Reynolds had experienced a vague, ill-defined feeling that Donald Schiff was somehow moving around behind his back, angling for Adam's job as creative director at Martin-Philbrick. And yet, oddly, he was probably the only person in the office who liked Donald Schiff. But he knew he would never know exactly why.

"Listen, Adam, I don't mean to play cat and mouse—if you'll pardon the expression—but why in the world would anyone want to throw poor tortured animals through your window at four in the morning?" Donald smiled his slyest smile. "I mean I could understand it if someone of my stature were attacked. The gifted are always abused. But someone like you . . . someone with the soul of a bourgeois. Someone of such self-evident mediocrity. I can't imagine anyone getting mad at you—or even concerned enough about you—to take such serious action."

Adam looked at Donald, and then straight through Donald, and decided he would play Donald's game for a little while. That would probably be the quickest way to get rid of him. "Maybe it was just a mistake," said Adam dryly.

"A mistake?" echoed Donald, his eyebrows arching emphatically in mock surprise.

"Yeah," said Adam, "maybe they were drunk or

stoned or something and just picked the wrong house. Things like that happen, I guess."

"Come now, Adam, no one could possibly mistake that Gothic castle of yours for any other house on the block."

"Look," snapped Adam bitterly, "what goddamn business is it of yours, anyway?"

"It's just that I worry about you, Adam. After all, what would we do around here without you?" Donald smiled. He knew he was winning. Adam stared at Donald, but said nothing for a full five seconds. Then Donald leaned forward on the sofa and spoke in a very soft and low and friendly voice: "What's the matter, Adam? Cat got your tongue?"

Adam kept staring at the thin, slightly balding man seated across from him.

"Look, Donald," he said, "when are you gonna find a nice young man and settle down?"

Adam was surprised by his own words. It was the first time in six years that he'd come out with any kind of a direct statement questioning Donald's sexual orientation. The fact that he had made the statement with Donald sitting less than five feet from him made the entire situation seem unreal. Donald's composure remained intact. He spoke softly.

"At least I don't have any strange pussy dropping in on me at four in the morning. So there." Donald Schiff stuck out his tongue.

The phone on Adam's desk punctuated Donald's gesture with a dull, buzzing sound, signaling an interoffice call. Adam picked up the phone. He blew a silent kiss at Donald who quickly pantomimed the actions of a man vomiting violently. It was Roger Martin on the phone. "Hey, Adam, how goes it? Can you drop by my office in a few minutes? Nothing urgent. Just a few loose ends I want to wrap up with you before I leave town this afternoon." Adam nodded into the receiver as if he believed that Roger Martin's all-seeing eyes could spot him seated at his desk. "Okay, Rog. Give me about five minutes."

Adam placed the receiver back in its cradle and, without looking up at Donald Schiff, spoke in a low monotone: "If you came in here to talk about business, I'll be back in about twenty minutes. If you came in here just to bust my balls, I'll be back in about twenty years. Try me then."

Donald Schiff became sullen. His light gray eyes were dull, wintry clouds drifting toward a distant horizon that existed somewhere high above Adam Reynolds's head. Bernie Stoneheim is right, thought Adam, the guy's an absolute fuckin' weirdo.

"Where are you going?" asked Donald soberly, his eyes still staring at some distant horizon only he could see.

"I'm going in to see Roger. He probably wants to speak to me about canning your ass."

Donald Schiff spoke: "Why that man trusts your judgment in creative affairs is perhaps the purest example of the blind leading the blind in modern history."

"Fuck you," said Adam, getting up from his desk and starting toward the door.

"Fuck you, too," said Donald, brushing back a wisp of stringy hair the color of common wrapping paper.

Adam walked out of the room without looking back. Donald Schiff sat staring into space for about twenty seconds. Then he spoke to the only person he truly trusted and admired. "The assholes. That's all they are, Donald, dear. Just absolute assholes."

CHAPTER 5

On the way to Roger Martin's office, Adam Reynolds found himself sinking into the soft, sticky pudding of self-pity that had become a constant part of his life lately. Maybe it was because he had just been with Donald Schiff. But more probably it was because he was going to see Roger Martin.

Adam wasn't envious of Roger. It was just that Roger Martin's success in business—president of Martin-Philbrick at the age of thirty-four, and now an important board member of a number of major corporations before forty—reminded Adam Reynolds that his own career had not only become rather ordinary, but that it had stopped moving forward a long time ago. And that it would never move forward again. Somehow, thought Adam, I went from a bright young kid with terrific potential to a middle-age guy going through the motions and counting out his life in coffee spoons. The shit part is that no one noticed it happening, not even me. When did it happen, he thought, was there a particular month, a particular year? Where did it go? The energy. The enthusiasm. The drive.

When you come right down to it, he thought, Roger is really a mediocre kind of person—except for one thing. Drive. The son of a bitch would push his mother's face in quicksand if it would help him make a few more bucks. It must be his lack of height. Typical small-man complex. Has to beat the shit out of everyone in the boardroom and the bedroom. He's not the brightest guy in the world. And clearly not the most talented or sensitive. There've got to be six or eight people right in this office with more brains and more on the ball than Roger Martin. And yet he's the boss. The big boss. He rings and I come running. It's such a horseshit way to make a living. I'm tired. I'm tired of Roger Martin. I'm tired of Donald Schiff. But most of all, I'm just tired of the whole fuckin' thing.

Adam knocked at Roger Martin's door. There was no answer. Adam remembered the time Roger Martin had boasted to him: "Adam, I just bought my wife a new set of tits. No kidding. Three thousand bucks for a silicone job. Or should I say two silicone jobs? Anyway, she feels like a new woman." Roger Martin had roared with laughter.

It had been Roger Martin's good fortune to have a number of clients who permitted him to build ad campaigns that featured exotic locales like Paris, Hawaii, Rumania, Tahiti, Buenos Aires, and many more. Roger always made it a point to supervise personally all photographic work in these locales, selecting local models on the basis of

their willingness to grant enthusiastic sexual fa-
vors to the man who had made it all possible. One
of the conditions of the models' unwritten con-
tracts was that immediately after performing an
especially exciting and gratifying sexual act with
Roger Martin, they would pose suggestively for
his own camera. The purpose of these photos was
that Roger Martin could have tangible evidence
of his masculinity to show to the art directors
and writers and account executives at Martin-
Philbrick. That's why he compiled a photo album
listing girls by countries. "It is my intention," he
announced to a small group in the office one day,
"to conquer the world. Some countries I may even
conquer six or seven times."

Adam was genuinely embarrassed by Roger
Martin's obsessive need to boast about his sexual
conquests. He was perhaps even more embarrassed, as he knocked again at Roger Martin's office door, by the realization that he had not been
with a woman himself for three months. And on
that occasion, it hadn't been a teenage student
grinning erotically into a camera. It had been a
forty-two-year-old department store buyer whom
Adam had met at an advertising party. They had
both drunk too much and somehow wound up at
her apartment and managed to get half of each
other's clothes off before consummating the deed
on the living-room sofa while Johnny Carson
laughed at them gleefully in the background.
Adam hadn't seen her again since that night. He
wasn't quite sure he'd recognize her if he did.

After Adam knocked on the door to Roger Martin's office for the third time, he realized no one was going to answer, so he opened the door and walked in. Gay—Roger Martin's private secretary—was not at her desk. Adam crossed the few steps from Gay's desk to the door to Roger Martin's private office. He knocked. No answer. Finally he opened the door and stepped into the room. Roger Martin was sitting in a huge, semireclining black swivel chair that was placed directly in back of a large marble desk. He was facing the door. And he was dead.

Adam was amazed at how quickly he realized that Roger Martin was dead. There was no need for Adam to feel Roger Martin's pulse. Or check his heartbeat. Or perform any of the rituals religiously followed on TV detective shows. Roger Martin's eyes said it all. They were wide-open and empty. And absolutely dead.

Adam realized that Roger Martin could only have been dead for a few moments. He also realized that from now on, Roger Martin would be dead forever.

Adam's hand was still gripping the doorknob. He stood staring at 145 pounds of useless, inert matter that sat pasty-faced and openmouthed, and marble-eyed, when only a few moments before it had been a whole galaxy of interrelated systems of valves and veins and nerves and glands that moved with energy and intelligence. And, Adam thought, with drive and determination. Where is the drive? Where is the determination now? Look at him. He looks stupid.

Adam's first clear thought was that Roger Martin, in death, reminded him of nothing so much as a huge squirrel: its marble eyes bulging, its skin taking on the gray complexion of a cold northern winter.

Adam didn't feel shock or grief or compassion or anything faintly resembling these emotions. He felt nothing more powerful than annoyance or inconvenience. This is going to be embarrassing, he thought. I'll have to notify the people in the office. And the family, of course. That's going to be a bitch. But then why should I have to notify the family? It's going to be bad enough putting up with the horseshit hysteria that's going to be going on around here. Oh, balls. Why did he have to die here? And why did he have to call me into his office just before he died? It was tough enough working for the prick. But at least that was strictly business. This is the man's death. It's too personal for me. I don't even really know him. He looks like an absolute stranger with his eyes like that. A squirrel, he looks like a goddamned stuffed squirrel.

Adam finally relaxed his grip on the doorknob and walked the six or seven steps that brought him directly in front of Roger Martin's desk. He realized it was time to do something practical, so he walked around the desk and took Roger Martin's left hand in his own two hands. With his fingers he fumbled along Roger Martin's left wrist, feeling for a pulse. Nothing.

He had seen people in the movies—and twice in real life—put their ears against a dying man's chest. And so he did the same. Again, nothing. He released Roger Martin's wrist, lifted his ear from the dead man's chest, and straightened up stiffly. There was nothing to do but notify the others.

The phone rang. For a second or two, a startled Adam Reynolds waited for Roger Martin to pick up the receiver. Then, as he remembered that Roger Martin would never again answer a phone call, Adam reached for the receiver. "Hello," he said softly, "Mr. Martin's office."

"Hello," a young boy's voice answered. "May I speak to my father, please?" Adam hesitated before answering. He tried to think of the right thing to say. "Just a second, please." And then Adam remembered that Roger Martin, as far as he knew, was the father of two horribly spoiled teenage daughters, but no sons. "Who is this?" he asked, thinking perhaps that a teenage girl might possibly sound like a young boy on the phone.

The young voice on the other end of the phone answered, "My name is Robert and I want to speak to my father." Adam guessed the boy's age to be about ten or eleven.

"I think you've got the wrong number, son. This is Martin-Philbrick Advertising."

The boy answered, "I know it is. My father works there."

The boy's voice sounded strangely familiar to Adam, as if he had heard it a long time ago, perhaps in a dream. There was something else about it, too.

A speech impediment of some kind that hampered the pronunciation.

"And what's your father's name, son?"

The boy giggled. "It's Daddy."

Adam was impatient. "Look, son, I've got an emergency here. I don't have time to play around, so just tell me your daddy's name or I'll have to hang up on you."

The ten- or eleven-year-old voice became serious. "Is he dead?"

Adam was stunned. "Is who dead?"

The boy answered, "The man in the office with you."

"Who is this?" Adam yelled. "How can you tell there's someone in this office with me?"

"I can tell," said the boy, "because I can tell."

Adam glanced at the window that looked directly out on an apartment building across the street.

"Are you across the street?" Adam was confused, his voice almost hysterical.

"Maybe," the boy answered. "Maybe I'm across the street. And maybe I'm not across the street. . . . My name is Robert. I want to speak to my father. His name is Adam Reynolds."

Adam suddenly slammed down the receiver in fright. That's when he saw the old, torn photograph lying under Roger Martin's right hand on the desk. It was the picture of a five- or six-year-old boy in a pullover sweater and short pants. Standing between his legs was a small Boston terrier. In the background was a car. It looked like an

Oldsmobile, an early sixties model. The boy was smiling, but there was something enigmatic about his smile. No, it wasn't his smile that was strange. It was his mouth. His lip. His upper lip. The boy had a harelip. Adam moved Roger Martin's dead right hand off the edge of the photograph. He turned the picture over. There, in the scrawling scribble of a five-year-old was a simple message: "Hi, Daddy. I miss you. Your son, Robert.

Adam picked up the photograph and put it in his breast pocket and stared out the window to the apartment building across the street. And he was quite certain that he was going mad.

CHAPTER 6

Winter, mean and hard as a hammer of ice, stung the small, thin man's toes and fingertips. He cursed the broken heater of the wretched gray Volkswagen and watched his breath become shivering puffs of fog that disappeared into the windshield. It must be about three fifteen, he thought. With any luck at all I'll freeze to death before five.

Outside, a sky of frozen ashes was deepening into the premature darkness which natives of upstate New York accept as a normal, everyday fact of life in late December.

The driver's toes curled back inside his boots. His foot moved forward on the accelerator and the silent skeletons of lifeless trees lining the lonely road came at him faster now.

The incredible thing, the small, thin man thought, is that I did this to myself. I left goddamn glorious days of sunshine and nights of warm, sweet honey in golden California to freeze my bony ass to death because I thought there was more of a challenge here. He smiled and felt the cold afternoon air crease his upper lip like a paper cut. Well, there is more of a challenge here. It's a goddamn challenge just to keep my testicles from turning into ice cubes.

There was the sign up ahead. It was familiar to him now. He knew that once he passed the sign he would turn left in one mile, cross over a small toll bridge that local legend said was once crossed by the headless horseman. Then he would continue for three open miles through barren countryside straight out of a Wyeth canvas. The darkness was closing fast now. But no matter. Soon he would be home. Home, of course, was one of the largest institutions of its kind in the free world. Two hundred and eighty acres of lakes and trees and winding paths and madness surrounded by a fourteen-foot iron fence decorated to create the illusion that this was not the kind of place where people who had never hurt other human beings were put away for as long as fifty or sixty years, or however long it might take to rehabilitate them or bury them or whatever.

The small, thin man thought that people arriving for the first time from the outside world might be inclined to believe that they had come upon a large college campus preparing for some type of winter festival. A wide asphalt road split the 280 acres down the middle, and was flanked on both sides by a variety of peripheral roads, each of which contained a number of buildings of assorted sizes and shapes and functions. There was a large administrative building, a laundry, a cafeteria, a power plant, and a series of three-story structures that seemed to spread over the campus in no particular pattern. These structures housed the permanent residents and also served as the site for nursing stations and doctors' offices and therapy rooms. Separating the buildings were outdoor basketball courts, bicycle paths, and simple, unadorned park benches.

There were eight small apartment buildings for resident faculty and several Quonset huts left over from World War II that housed 130 cooks, electricians, carpenters, cleaning women, and other assorted personnel required to service and maintain a mental institution with some six thousand beds.

The gray Volkswagen creaked to a halt at the entrance gate to the property. A black-clad security guard stepped quickly out of a vertical coffin and stuck his face up close to the window on the driver's side of the car. Martin Kiernam stuck the fingers of his glove into his left armpit and pulled his hand free. It's already frozen solid, he thought, so what's the difference? He rummaged around in the glove compartment for a second or two and then produced a staff identification card which he held up to the window for the security guard to see.

"Go ahead, Doctor," the security guard said in a high-pitched voice that died quickly in the painfully cold air.

Martin Kiernam moved his gloveless hand to the gearshift, and the gray Volkswagen coughed twice then hurried toward Avenue C, where Martin Kiernam would park the car, walk fifty feet to

Faculty Residential Building C, and climb one flight of stairs to apartment 2D.

The minute Martin Kiernam parked the car, he saw the first snowflakes. By the time he reached Faculty Residential Building C, he thought it would be a four-star snow. Martin had devised his own system for rating upstate New York snowfalls. One star was a light, sugary powder that simply grazed the gray sidewalks for an hour or so and then was gone. A two-star snowfall could mean the appearance of sleighs and galoshes and tire chains. Three stars meant an hour or two of shoveling and spreading ashes. But four stars: four stars meant snowplows and closed schools and strangled traffic and maybe even four or five snow-related deaths reported in the *Buffalo News*. Of course, he couldn't be sure it was going to be four stars. It would be hours before he could be certain. But the wind had become a razor slicing out of the east. The snow was coming hard and fierce and sticking fast to the ground. Oh, why, in God's name, had he ever left California? Helping mankind was one thing, but freezing your ass off was another. Martin Kiernam climbed the stairs with winter in his soul. And with each step, he thought the same thought over and over. Fuck mankind, brother Martin, fuck mankind and pour the brandy.

Even before he set foot in his door, Martin Kiernam reached his hand along the pebbled surface of the wall and hit the light switch. The patients were considered relatively harmless, not the kind to sneak into a staff psychiatrist's apartment while he was out, and then cut his throat the minute he walked in the door. None of the patients had ever done anything like that. Well, maybe once or twice. But that was ages ago. Still, Martin Kiernam took certain precautions. After all, he reasoned, when you live alone you can't be too careful. People living in condominiums in Westchester and on farms in Iowa get their throats cut all the time. And here I am, living all by myself, literally surrounded by six thousand of the craziest people on earth.

As soon as he removed his heavy woolen jacket and gloves, Martin Kiernam poured himself a good three ounces of cognac. He gulped it down greedily, as if he had suddenly come upon an oasis in the Sahara, then quickly poured another ounce, as the slow fire started to build from the pit of his stomach and spiraled out in warming circles to his arms, legs, toes, fingers, and finally to the tips of his ears. Good, he thought, I'm going to live.

Martin Kiernam constantly worried about life and death in general, and his own life and death in particular. This obsession with the idea of his own human frailty, his own mortality, had more to do with the selection of psychiatry as a profession than any innate sense of compassion or concern for his fellowman. Even as a little boy of seven or eight, Martin Kiernam viewed each day not as an adventure to be pursued or an experience to be enjoyed, but rather as a menace to be survived. "Electric plugs can kill you if you touch them wrong. Never use the toilet anyplace but home. God knows what kind of germs you'll pick up. I don't care what the other kids' mothers let them do. I lost one baby, I'm not going to lose you." Martin Kiernam's mother had died the day Richard Nixon was elected President, choking to death at her kitchen table on a particularly stringy piece of veal parmigiana. Further proof to Martin Kiernam that no one and nothing, not even veal and especially veal parmigiana, was ever to be trusted again. Of course, he had the intelligence and professional insight to cope with his mother now, especially since she was gone. But some days she could give him a terrific battle. And today was one of those days. "That's really smart, Martin. I mean, you're a doctor, a smart-ass psychiatrist, and you still don't have the brains to get the heater in your car fixed good before you go for a drive. But you know what, before you die of pneumonia, you'll get yourself squished like chopped meat in that little paper car you drive. That little toy couldn't stand up if a three-wheel bike ran into it at six miles an hour. But go ahead. Throw your life away. Outside of your father, you're the last Kiernam left."

The brandy surrounded and seduced the winter winds that had buried themselves in Martin Kiernam's shoulders and arms and legs. He felt the threat of death subsiding. In the warmth of his apartment, Martin Kiernam's mother's voice left her son alone to sip a solitary brandy and wonder seriously if he was just kidding himself that he was helping anyone here. That's not true, he thought, I've helped myself some just by coming here, just by breaking away from California. And there are patients we do help. I mean even if we don't rehabilitate some of them to the point where they can go back into the real world, at least we help them cope better with their situation here than they could on the outside.

He thought of the two middle-aged brothers who had been as inseparable during their thirty years inside the fence as they had been during their fifteen years outside. It was imaginative, Martin thought, the way their father punished them. Insane, but imaginative. What he did, simply, was paint the boys' room black. Not just the walls. But the ceiling and the floors. And the closets and the windows. And the furniture. And the doors. Everything. Black. A private universe of total darkness. No way of knowing time or the passage of time. The boys were in there for a long while together, and so they grew closer to each other than one would expect brothers to be. They held hands constantly. They slept in the same bed. They ate from the same plate. They stumbled and groped and grasped their way to becoming lovers. And all the time they never saw the sun or a tree or a door or each other's faces or anything, anything at all. Just blackness. Blackness for a period estimated at six years and four months. But the boys deserved such punishment. After all, they had gone to a movie without their father's permission. And if he let them get away with that, God knows what they'd try next. After the father died and the boys were discovered cowering naked against a black wall, they were immediately brought to the institution in upstate New York. Thirty years they've been here together, thought Martin, just eight less years than I've been alive. They'll never get better. They can't ever get better. But at least here they can see the sunshine. And they won't wind up slashing some poor kid's throat or raping some housewife. They still cry sometimes at night when the lights are turned off. But they're better off in here. At least in here, someone cares for them.

And what about the redheaded woman who had been virtually catatonic for twenty years?

The redheaded woman was Martin Kiernam's favorite patient. Not because she was making progress (she wasn't), nor because she never caused any problems (she did), but because she was simply the most fascinating and puzzling case Martin Kiernam had ever had the opportunity to work with.

He had been with her for six months now, and soon he would give a detailed report on her to a large group of psychiatric students who spent one full year at the institution in order to observe classroom studies in reality, and to work firsthand on therapy programs with manageable patients. He imagined his next lecture.

"This is our patient," he began. The thin, pale, redheaded woman stared blankly at the tiers of white-jacketed students who sat facing her from a darkened distance of thirty feet. "She is, as Winston Churchill once said of Russia, a puzzle wrapped inside an enigma! About twenty years ago, she did something rather startling for a young married woman. It was on Christmas Day. She was preparing a big turkey dinner for her husband and some guests—their next-door neighbors, another young married couple. It seems that while her husband and the others were in the living room having a bit of Christmas cheer, she took her new electric carving knife—a Christmas gift from her husband—and instead of carving up the turkey, she very neatly sliced off both her breasts."

A few audible sighs and the sound of painful cringes slipped through the audience. The redheaded woman stared into the darkness, the shadowy white figures accented by the soft glow of cigarettes.

"Now," Martin Kiernam continued, "what makes a beautiful twenty-two-year-old girl with no history of mental problems suddenly mutilate herself so horribly and, of course, permanently? By the way, I think that's a key word here. Permanently. I think our patient wanted to inflict a punishment on herself that could not be cured, could not be corrected. It's my best guess that she didn't commit suicide because she felt suicide would be too quick, too easy. She wanted to suffer. And suffer for the rest of her life. And she also wanted to destroy herself as a woman.

"Now. How do I know this to be true?" Martin

Kiernam looked up from his notes and glanced at the pathetic white-gowned creature sitting silently in a chair about ten feet to his left. "I don't. I don't know if any of it is true. She has never told us very much. But I think I can put together a pretty good case for my thesis. Be sure you take notes on this. You may be questioned on it later. In any event, I will want to hear your prognosis, your suggestions, your concepts. Who knows? Perhaps one of you will have an insight into the particular madness that lives in her, and can help lead the rest of us on a course of positive action. Let us hope so."

Martin Kiernam paused, took a quick nervous sip from a glass of water, and turned a page in his notes. "By the way," he went on, "please don't think I've gone back to medieval mental brutality by having the patient present while we discuss her case. For one thing, we're extremely doubtful she will hear anything I say. She just tunes herself out automatically. And for another thing, it might not be the worst thing in the world for her to hear her case being discussed. Nothing has worked very well in twenty years. So we don't have very much to lose." He paused again for emphasis.

"Now," he went on, "let me give you my ideas on why this woman came here in the first place. And why I believe she will never leave.

"Our records show that she was born March 15, 1935, in the Bronx, New York—the second child of an Irish Catholic couple we'll call Edward and Kathleen. Their first child, a boy, named Danny, had died years earlier at the age of eight." Martin Kiernam thought quickly of his own dead baby sister, a girl he had never seen, a girl who had died at the age of sixteen months when she smothered in her own bedcovers. Her name was Amy, and even though he had never seen or touched the little girl, she had been a part of Martin Kiernam's life for as long as he could remember.

"I think it's important that we understand a bit about her parents and how her brother died. It was winter and Danny and some of his friends had been hitching their sleighs to the backs of buses for free rides around the neighborhood. The bus Danny had been hanging onto skidded suddenly. Danny lost his grip and his sleigh shot forward, directly under the rear wheels of the bus. The wheels went right over the young boy's head, crushing his skull and smashing his face beyond recognition. When the bus came to a stop, all the passengers hurried off to see what had happened. Kathleen, the boy's mother, happened to be one of the passengers. She recognized the long blue and white wool sweater she had knit for her son.

"For a long time after Danny's death—and this was revealed by our patient's father at the time she was admitted—the dead boy's mother would dream that she was back in Ireland walking barefoot through a meadow covered with fresh fallen snow. Somehow her feet never felt the cold. Everything in the dream seemed pure and beautiful. But then the snow began to melt, and as it melted it slowly began to change from white to pink to vivid red. And Kathleen found herself sinking into the red snow. And as she felt her body slipping beneath the snow, she could hear a young boy's voice. It was Danny. He was crying that he was cold. God only knows how many times Kathleen dreamed that dream."

Martin Kiernam gazed at his audience, and his audience gazed back. There was absolute silence.

"Now. The father didn't turn to dreams. No. The father turned to drink. It seems as if he drank every day. He was a construction laborer. He drank on the job. He drank after work. And he drank in the morning before work."

Martin Kiernam paused to search his audience's reaction in the semidarkness. He put his notes down on the podium stand, and slowly started to walk toward the spot where the patient was seated, talking a little more softly as he walked, holding a portable microphone in his hand, tugging occasionally at the wire that trailed behind.

"Almost twelve years to the day Danny was buried," he went on, "our patient was born. By that time the father had forgotten why it was he drank so heavily. And the mother had stopped having those dreams. But instead of bringing new life into her parents' home, the baby girl brought only a reminder of pain. She entered the world not as a person in her own right, but as a prisoner of a split second in time twelve years earlier when a New York City bus had skidded on an icy street. Obviously it was not a good way to begin life. But it was a beginning."

Martin Kiernam could feel the words flowing freely now, confident that he was not only informing students about the patient, but also fascinating them with his fluid presentation and penchant for the dramatic.

"Surely," he challenged his audience, "you have heard the cliché that time heals all wounds. I submit that it merely disguises them. Gradually the mother began to spend less and less time fingering the beads of her rosary and more and more time making pretty little dresses for the pretty little girl. And the father reached a point where he could remain sober for two or three weeks at a stretch. And there were even times when he would play hide-and-seek with her or take her for walks, or read her to sleep.

"But Kathleen and Edward could never bring themselves to the point where they truly loved their daughter. Oh, they liked her well enough, indeed. But they realized that liking someone very much was quite different and far less dangerous than loving someone too much."

Martin Kiernam looked up from his notes and spoke directly to his audience.

"By the time the girl had reached the age of fourteen, she had become an astonishingly lovely young woman, although her beauty was delicate and classic and oddly out of place and time amid the vigorous bustle of neighborhood life in the Bronx.

"As an only child—or rather as the only surviving child of parents who by now had settled into passive middle age—she never experienced the give-and-take and petty jealousies and shared joys and hurts that are as much a part of life to children with brothers and sisters as is brushing their teeth in the morning or battling over toys or getting chicken pox one after the other."

Martin Kiernam turned another page of notes. "And because her parents had left their families in Ireland, she had no cousins or aunts or uncles or grandparents to visit and play with and stay with on holidays and summer vacations.

"It is not strange, then, that the girl grew up not caring very much for people. It wasn't that she didn't like them. She just never seemed to care about them very much one way or the other. People were all right, as long as they let her be, as long as they didn't expect anything of her. She much preferred the company of animals and babies. Her parents wouldn't let her have a pet—although she often begged them. They weren't being mean. They just wanted to spare her the heartbreak of seeing a little kitten or puppy crushed under the wheels of a bus on one of the streets in the busy neighborhood. But they did let their daughter baby-sit for neighbors, and the hours she spent baby-sitting were probably the happiest of her youth. She was paid twenty-five cents an hour, but would gladly have done it for free."

Martin Kiernam could sense a growing restlessness in his audience. The whispers of cloth brushing against cloth as legs crossed and uncrossed.

The quick clearing of a throat. The faint tapping of a pencil against paper. He looked up from his notes and out at his audience, staring them into silence.

"So much for the early years. I just wanted to give you a basic sketch, a background, so to speak, of the early environment our patient experienced. Let's look at her now at the age of twenty-one.

"A college senior, majoring in English. Quiet. Fine student. No boyfriends, in spite of her exceptional good looks. Described by classmates as intelligent but inaccessible. A loner. Probably a virgin. Apparently unconcerned about religion or politics. Then she meets someone, perhaps the first adult she responds to with any degree of enthusiasm. A young man just a few years older than she. Tall. Husky. The outgoing type. Just starting out in business." Martin Kiernam paused for effect. "You know the rest of the story. He is completely taken by her beauty, her quiet intelligence, the softness of her manner. She seems to react to his energy, his humor, his drive. He brings her out of herself into his world. They date. They go steady. They're engaged and married all within a period of nine weeks. It's the old opposites-attract and roller-coaster courtship made famous by M-G-M. Shy girl, go-getter guy, hearts, flowers, the patter of little footsteps. Doris Day and Rock Hudson happiness forever after. Only that isn't the way it worked. They had been married only a short time when things began to come apart.

"He was offered a promising position in Florida

which thrilled them both. And so, happy as a couple of kids on the last day of school before summer vacation, they packed their bags and headed South—to Miami. Fortunately, he already had a few friends living there, so they didn't arrive as absolute strangers."

Martin Kiernam glanced over at his patient and thought for a second that she must look like one of those corpses that had been quick-frozen at death. She didn't blink. She didn't seem to be breathing. She isn't alive, thought Martin.

He continued: "Things went well for them in Florida. His career moved forward rapidly. They made a number of new friends. They bought a big old house in a fine residential community, and then the best news of all—she became pregnant. And then it all started to unravel.

"One morning during the middle stages of the pregnancy—say about the eighteenth week—our patient woke up to discover a small, bright-red rash on her face. At first she thought it was nothing. Probably something she had eaten. But as the day progressed, the rash began to deepen and spread. By noon, it had reached her neck and shoulders. She became quite worried and phoned her husband at work. He hurried home and by the time he arrived, his beautiful young wife looked like something you might see in a horror movie. Her delicate features were partially hidden behind a series of rough red welts that seemed to be lengthening and thickening by the moment. The welts—or rash—became unbearably itchy—and the girl had all she could do to keep from clawing her skin off."

Martin Kiernam took a sip of water and turned another page of his notes.

"She was taken to one dermatologist. Then another. Then another. They all took tests. They all prescribed treatments. But nothing worked. Within a week, the girl was literally a mass of blotchy red scar tissue from head to toe. And her condition worsened with the passing of each day.

"She was admitted to a hospital where the head dermatologist was considered to be one of the two or three foremost authorities in his field in the entire country. He had, in fact, been the government's top consultant on tropical diseases during World War II. He, and a team of specialists, conducted the most exhaustive battery of tests you can imagine trying to track down the root cause of the rash. They confessed to absolute failure."

Martin Kiernam closed his notebook and spoke in a less formal tone to his audience. "I'm going to ask your indulgence here, for a moment or two. What I'd like to do is very quickly recreate some scenes between the dermatologist and the patient's husband. Now, these scenes may never have actually taken place. But chances are something like them did. And chances are they went something like this."

Martin Kiernam changed his attitude, his posture. His storytelling ability made it possible for him to bring events of long ago vividly back to life in his students' minds. Suddenly he was traveling across the years to a hospital office in Florida. And he was hoping the students were making the trip with him.

"I've never seen anything like it," said the head dermatologist to the husband. "It looks like a weird variation of rubella, but it doesn't react to treatment like rubella. There are some things we could try, some new miracle drugs we could use, but I'm afraid of the devastating side effects they might have on her baby."

"To hell with the baby," answered the husband, "the baby isn't even born yet. But if you don't stop this thing soon, I think it's going to drive her crazy. And me, too. I just can't stand here and watch her like this."

"You want us to try the drugs?" the doctor asked.

"I want you to try anything that will make my wife well," answered the husband.

The doctor spoke: "We've got a real problem there. Your wife doesn't want us to try the drugs. She said she doesn't want us to use anything that could hurt her baby. And the fact is, that while your wife is suffering very much right now, her life is in no immediate danger. If she doesn't want us to use the drugs, for fear it'll hurt her baby, well, then there's no way we can use the drugs. Unless you can get her to change her mind."

"What happens if you don't use these new drugs?"

The doctor shrugged. "We can't say for sure.

The whole thing might dry up and go away on its own as quickly as it came on. It's possible that it's a psychosomatic condition. Brought on by nerves. Anxiety. Perhaps even an unconscious fear of the responsibility of being a mother, of being responsible for another's life."

The husband was certain that couldn't be so. "Look, Doctor, I know the human mind can play strange tricks on us and all that. But if there's one thing I know, it's that my wife wants to have a baby. I mean she really wants it."

The doctor rubbed the bridge of his nose with a stubby forefinger. "I don't doubt that consciously your wife wants the baby. And I rather suspect that unconsciously she also wants the baby. I'm not a psychiatrist. And I really don't think your wife's problem is psychological. I just say we have to recognize that it's a possibility. I believe her problem is organic. Some virus we haven't been able to isolate. You know, there are as many skin conditions as you can possibly imagine. It could be a virus alone. Or it could be a virus acting in combination with some chemical your wife has been exposed to. By itself, the chemical might not be harmful. By itself, the virus might not be harmful. Together, they might be devastating. And the unique thing here is that they might only be devastating for your wife. You might come in contact with the same elements and they would have no effect on you."

The husband listened intently.

"It could be anything. Or any combination of

things. Viruses. Chemicals. The season of the year. A food. A soap. Your wife's emotional makeup. Her physical condition. Her physical condition complicated by pregnancy. It's a complex puzzle and we haven't fit all the pieces together. We know a few things that it is not. But we don't know what it is. And we may never know what it is."

The husband stared at the doctor. "If you don't know what it is, then why do you want to use those new drugs?"

The doctor hesitated, then spoke slowly: "Because I don't know what else to do, what else we can do. And frankly, I'm just hoping that we might get lucky. There's a good chance the drugs might work for your wife. I've seen them clear up other conditions we couldn't diagnose with any degree of certainty. That's why we call them wonder drugs. But, of course, there's one problem."

"One problem?"

"The drugs may have a most beneficial effect on your wife. But they may have a most devastating effect on her child."

"I don't see that we have a choice," said the husband.

"I don't see that it's our choice," answered the doctor. "It's hers."

Martin Kiernam had temporarily finished playing the dual roles of noted dermatologist and worried husband.

He spoke in his own voice. "If there is one particular thing that plunged this woman's mind into a solitary prison where it has existed in anguish for the last twenty years, you have just heard it. Do you know what that key is? Here. I'll repeat it."

Once again, he became the dermatologist. "I don't see that it's our choice," he repeated. "It's hers."

Now the voice was Martin Kiernam's. "Hers. Her choice. Her decision. Her responsibility. And how many people have hidden behind a catatonic cloud of silence—hidden forever—because they couldn't face or couldn't escape a reality that was too painful for them to live with?

"In the weeks after the meetings with the dermatologist, the husband literally got down on his hands and knees and pleaded with his wife to take the special drugs. By now, her features were totally indistinguishable behind the raw, raised blotches that covered her face and body. This was an extraordinarily beautiful young woman whose appearance was now as bad or worse than the mutilated survivors of Hiroshima. She was absolutely hideous. No mirrors were allowed in her room for fear the shock of her own appearance might do her permanent mental or emotional damage. No visitors were allowed, save her husband. Finally, the husband told her what a lot of you have probably been thinking right along. That she was being totally absurd, absolutely ridiculous for allowing herself to suffer like this for some nameless, shapeless piece of protoplasm buried in her body. For God's sake, it was one thing to want a child. He could understand that. But this. This was insane. It was destroying her. It was destroying him. And he just couldn't take it any longer. He literally got down on his knees and begged her to try the drugs.

"She consented. One day later, the first of the new wonder drugs was administered. Within four days, the redness of the blotches started to subside. Within a week, some of the welts began to shrink slightly. Within two weeks, her features were once again discernible. She was allowed to have a mirror. Her husband came to visit her with a much lighter heart and a happy smile on his face and cheering tales about how they would make up for lost time after she had the abortion and how they then could have other children.

"She had thought it over, she told him, and she had decided to have the baby. At first, realizing the ordeal she had just been through, the young husband was sympathetic and understanding toward her feelings. Slowly and without asserting any undue pressure, he described the possible effects the new drugs might have on their unborn child. The baby might be born blind, he told her. There was a chance it could be born with no legs. Or no arms. It could certainly be retarded. It might have a faulty heart. Or an upside-down stomach. Or any of a thousand and one other disastrous disabilities that would not only make life extremely difficult for the baby, but would also place an incredible strain on their marriage and perhaps prevent them from having healthy, normal babies in the future simply because they couldn't afford other children due to the enormous costs of caring for a child that would be a medical freak.

"The wife listened to the husband's arguments but then told him that she had also been talking to some doctors and that some of them felt she had a good chance of giving birth to a reasonably normal child. They all said that there were risks, of course. There was no way of telling exactly how much damage the new drugs might have done to the fetus, but the chance for a normal delivery might be as high as seventy-five percent in her favor.

"I don't like the odds." Once again Martin Kiernam was assuming the voice of the young husband. "We've got the rest of our lives in front of us and we could wreck them for good if we play roulette and that baby is born deaf and dumb. Sure, it could be born beautiful and as healthy and normal as both of us. But, honey, what if it isn't? My God, I've got a career ahead of me. We've got our whole lives in front of us. Honey, honey, believe me. It just isn't worth the risk."

Martin Kiernam was caught up in the drama and couldn't bring himself to acknowledge that it was time for a ten-minute break.

"Remember," he went on in his own voice, "this was twenty years ago. Abortions were illegal. Many people—not just Right to Life crusaders, but perhaps even a majority of the population—looked at abortion as something bordering on murder. Oh, people went ahead and had them by the hundreds of thousands, but there generally was a feeling of shame and sin and loss and death surrounding them. And remember, too, that this girl was raised a Roman Catholic. Even though she wasn't married in the Church and wasn't a practicing Catholic at the time of these events, it seems evident that her early religious training probably had a powerful, perhaps even overpowering effect on her attitude, her resistance.

"But finally that resistance broke down. And it broke down not only because of the pleading of her young husband, but because of the advice of most of the doctors familiar with the case. Now, of course, abortion being illegal at that time—even therapeutic abortions unless the mother's very life was at stake—the physicians didn't come right out and professionally advise abortion. But they could make statements like this: 'As a doctor, I cannot and will not recommend abortion. It's against the law and it's as simple as that. But as a man, I can say that I'm not sure I'd want to risk bringing a child into the world who could ruin my own life and my wife's. Not to mention the suffering for the child. There'll always be time for other children.'

"Of all the doctors they spoke to in confidence—and it was probably a dozen—only one was really against the whole idea of abortion. Others pointed out the possibility that the child might be born perfectly normal, but they were either indecisive or unconvincing as to whether they'd take the risk. Except this one young doctor. An Englishman. An obstetrician on staff at the hospital where our patient was staying. A very intense, very forceful, very convincing person. He was one hundred percent against abortion. And he made no bones about it."

Once again, Martin Kiernam slipped into character.

"Religion has nothing to do with it. If anything, I'm probably a practicing agnostic. But I do know this as sure as I'm sitting here. Life exists in your womb this very minute. It is growing, eating, developing. It can either go on growing, eating, developing until it is delivered as a human being in its own right. Or it can be destroyed. The choice is yours, of course. There are places you can go to have an abortion. Illegally in this country. But legally, and under medical supervision, in other countries.

"Now. You've been asking me about statistics. About what the percentages are that your baby will be born normal."

Martin Kiernam paused, lit a cigarette, and blew a thin stream of white smoke toward his audience. The English doctor spoke again.

"No one can really say what is going to happen for sure. But this much we do know with absolute certainty. If you decide to have an abortion, the baby, or fetus, or protoplasm, or whatever you want to call it will have no chance at all. None. Zero. Abortion is absolute. There's no changing your mind.

"There's another problem, of course. You're far

enough along in your pregnancy—twenty-two or twenty-three weeks, I should say—that an abortion will not be as simple as it might have been a month or two ago.

"By the way, you can feel the baby inside you a little, can't you? Do you know what he looks like now? Let me tell you. He's about twelve inches long. He already has hair. Even eyebrows. He's putting on weight, getting the chubby look of the newborn. His hands, feet, toes, fingers are already perfectly formed.

"I don't mean to shock or disturb you, but I do think you should know what will happen to you and the life within you if you should decide to have an abortion. A few weeks ago, they could have done it with a simple salt solution. This means they would take a heavy-gauge needle and insert it through your stomach and uterus and into your amniotic sac. That's the fluid-filled sac that surrounds the fetus. Or baby. Then they draw out about a half-pint of amniotic fluid and replace it by a heavily concentrated salt solution. Now at this point in the pregnancy, the fetus is already breathing on a system something like a skin diver with an Aqua-lung. He breathes in the poisonous salt solution, swallows it, struggles, and expires. It takes about an hour to kill him. Unfortunately, we don't believe it is painless for the fetus. About a day later, you should go into labor and deliver your 'terminated pregnancy.' Once, in a very great while, the fetus is delivered live, but dies soon after.

"However, because of the late stage of your pregnancy, you will have a hysterotomy. It is a good bit more dangerous than the salt method. And there's a far greater chance of the fetus being born alive. It's like a cesarean, actually. The incision is smaller. It's all really quite simple. What happens is the doctor—if you go to a qualified doctor—reaches into the uterus, detaches the placenta from the uterine wall, and removes the fetus. Now if this were a true cesarean section, the doctor would hand the baby quickly to the attending nurse, who would get the phlegm out of the baby's nose and mouth to get it breathing as quickly as possible. The baby would then be rushed into the newborn nursery, where every possible effort would be made to save its life. In the hysterotomy abortion, however, no such effort is made. The fetus is cut free and then held inside the mother until it suffocates. Or it simply is deposited in a bucket where it dies. These fetuses have been observed to live for two or three hours after the actual operation. Two or three hours, all the while struggling frantically for survival. And doctors and nurses stand around and watch them struggle and do absolutely nothing to help them. In fact, in most cases, they take what they feel are humane measures to shorten the period of struggle. It's been done for years."

Once again Martin Kiernam stepped from his actor's role to assume command of his audience. "I hope you can see what I'm trying to accomplish here. If I told you this woman went into a catatonic state a few months after having an illegal abortion, she becomes another sad statistic. But if I can get you to feel a bit of the confusion, some of the personal anguish she must have felt, we may learn something. Here was a fragile, relatively isolated woman coming off a horrible emotional and physical experience that in itself could destroy a stronger person's equilibrium. Now she is faced with what to her amounted to a life-and-death decision. And instead of having a sympathetic physician holding her hand and explaining clearly and logically the soundness of the decision to seek an abortion, she is confronted with a doctor who doesn't have to have the baby, who won't have to spend thirty or forty years with a mongoloid or deaf and dumb human being with the intelligence level of a Labrador retriever. And this doctor very clearly and very coldly puts in this sensitive young girl's mind that if she has the abortion, she will, in fact, be a murderess.

"The abortion was performed on a Caribbean island where such operations were legal and properly supervised. But the circumstances surrounding the operation were hideous in regard to what they must have done to the young girl's mind. First off, she had to flee the country, her own country, as if she were a common criminal. Second, her face and body were still covered to a good degree with thick red welts, and where the welts had subsided, with pinkish shadows that would leave their mark for a year or longer. On the flight, she wore large, dark sunglasses, a black sweater, black slacks, and black gloves—hardly the typical tourist wardrobe you'd expect to see on a Caribbean vacation. Naturally, she attracted the attention and curious stares of the other passsengers, increasing the incredibly powerful feeling of guilt that was probably the dominant fact in her mental attitude at that time.

"Then it was done. Quickly. Impersonally. By an unknown doctor in a strange hospital in a foreign country. The husband was supremely happy, of course. Now they could get back to normal and he could get on with his career. The only problem was that four and one-half months later, on the day her gynecologist had predicted she would give birth—Christmas Day, to be precise—the young woman took an electric carving knife, slashed off her breasts, and presented them to her husband and their guests on a silver serving tray that had been a wedding gift."

Martin Kiernam shook his head slowly. He spoke to his audience in a whisper. "Merry Christmas," he said.

CHAPTER 7

The moon was a naked light bulb staring back
from eternity and down, down at his eyes like the
hot, blinding beam interrogators use to confuse
and frighten suspects into confession. Frogs chat-
tered in a curious monotone, asking questions that
made more sense than the fragmented thoughts
moving slowly around in Adam Reynolds's mind,
trying to attach themselves to one another to form
a single idea, a thread of logic, a pattern that
made sense.

The orange tip of a cigarette glowed like a tiny
planet of fire in the blackness of the back porch.
Off in the distance, a dog barked. Overhead, a
throaty jet purred its approach to Miami Interna-
tional Airport. Adam Reynolds bent his head
slightly to the right and looked at the luminous
dials of his watch. Ten minutes to three. Or was it
three minutes to ten? And what difference did it
make? Time was unimportant, of course. Time
had become increasingly unimportant for Adam
Reynolds since . . . since . . . he couldn't remember exactly since when. He couldn't remem-

ber how long it had been since he had felt like eating a meal or going to work or even changing his bed sheets. He still did these things, of course. And other things, hundreds of other things, like brushing his teeth and moving his bowels and shopping for groceries. Because somehow Adam Reynolds knew that these things were expected of him. And so he did them without passion or purpose, making his daily life a pantomime of the routine his life had hardened into over the years. "Two eggs over easy with hash browns and bacon," he would say. And then he would cover the eggs and potatoes in a crimson pool of catsup as he had done practically every morning for the last ten years. And then he would eat his breakfast, but he wouldn't taste it. He would smile at the waitress, but wouldn't see her. He would sit there alone at a table in the Ranch House Restaurant on Coral Way with only his breakfast and the morning edition of the *Miami Herald* for company, and he would wonder why people thought it was important to talk to each other, and make plans and attend meetings and go to movies and buy insurance and change underwear and go through the whole foolish routine of wasted motion and empty words, over and over, again and again. It was all so useless and senseless and futile and empty and finally so horribly and tediously boring. This is what makes sense, thought Adam, his eyes fixed on a pale white globe that hovered a few hundred thousand miles above his back porch. The moon makes sense, thought Adam. The moon really makes sense.

And then it came. Just as it had come every night for as long as Adam Reynolds could remember. It always came about this time, between 2:30 and 3:15 every morning.

It was the phone call. The one constant in Adam Reynolds's life. Sometimes he answered it. Sometimes he didn't. Sometimes he shouted obscenities into the receiver as loudly as he could. Other times he simply took the receiver off the hook and went straight up to bed, where he would wait for the sun to pour through his window and tell him it was time to get up and go to work.

Adam Reynolds breathed in the sweet night air of the back porch. A quick, bold breeze brushed through branches of poinsettias and palms, the soft, natural sound underscoring the hard, shrill, nervous whine of the ringing phone.

Why not, thought Adam, why not chat a bit? There's not much else to do around here tonight.

It took almost all of his will, but Adam managed to uncross his long, slender legs from the stationary position they had been in for three hours.

Adam placed his hands in front of him, palms down on the mahogany table, and pushed against its surface, rising slowly in the process. Then he opened the gateway doors that separated the back porch from the living room. He moved through the darkened living room like an old ship navigating through familiar but perilous waters.

He moved slowly. But he knew exactly where he was going.

He moved through the living room and into the foyer, and then finally, after a journey that seemed to cover hundreds of miles, he reached the phone.

Adam Reynolds sat in the swivel chair in front of the rolltop desk. He stared for a second down at the Cuban tile floor and thought he could feel himself slipping down inside the patterns that changed from flowers to faces to stars, and he was afraid that if he slipped down into the patterns, he might never get out of them. But maybe that wouldn't be too bad, either. He picked up the phone. "Hello," he said, his voice calm, almost friendly, "I've been expecting you."

CHAPTER 8

Dom Petrella was a bit on edge as he slid onto the familiar barstool and ordered a "dry vodka martini with no vermouth." It had been a month, maybe six weeks, since he had seen Adam Reynolds, and he wondered what could have happened during that time to make his friend sound so obviously and deeply troubled. The incident with the cats was upsetting, but Dom doubted that it would have had a lasting and serious effect on Adam. After all, Dom reasoned, Adam was the original "bounce-back kid," one of those resilient personalities who take direct hits from life and come back strong.

And yet Adam's voice, when he had called Dom to arrange for the lunch date, was a voice Dom had never heard before. It was flat and empty, and there was a quiet sense of fear.

The first quick, nervous sip of the vermouthless martini wet the edges of his black and bushy Zapata mustache. Before Dom placed his drink back on the bar, he felt the familiar friendly squeeze of a thumb and forefinger on the back of his neck. "Let me guess," he said. "Raquel Welch? No. No.

Lon Chaney, Jr.? Ah. I've got it. The immortal, the ever-popular Helmut Dantine." He glanced over his shoulder to see a faintly smiling Adam Reynolds in the dim, almost dusklike light of the Yorkshire Inn. Dom spoke again. "I was right. It's the infamous Nazi himself." Adam released his grip on Dom's neck and let his fingers slide slowly over and off the man's massive back. He sat on the barstool next to his companion's. He shook Dom's hand, then asked the bartender, Hank, for an extra-dry Beefeater martini with two or three olives.

"I thought you were cutting out martinis and sticking to Scotch?" asked Dom, his eyes making a fast analysis of the changes that had taken place in his friend since he'd seen him last. The features were the same, and then again they weren't. They were more agitated, more strained. The mouth was tight, clenched. The eyes were tired, empty. The smile, thought Dom, was as phony as a three-dollar bill.

As they were finishing their first round of martinis, Dom coughed, crushed out a little cigar in an otherwise spotless ashtray, and said, "Do you want to talk about it now?"

"I guess."

Dom slid a thick finger across his mustache. "Here?"

Adam pushed his empty glass in the general direction of the bartender who was busy taking the orders of a thirtyish couple seated about five empty barstools away from Adam and Dom.

"Here is as good a place as any, I guess. Although I don't know how to begin and I'm certain you'll believe I'm insane, and the fact of the matter is that there's an excellent chance that I am. Insane, that is."

"Shit, you've always been a bit strange in the brain, Reynolds. Everyone knows that. It's part of your charm." Dom smiled. Adam didn't.

The bartender was busy now mixing up another batch of martinis. "How long we know each other, Dom? Twenty, twenty-five years?" Adam's face was stiff, cold, frightened.

Dom answered, "Twenty-five years, at least."

Adam went on: "I'm serious now, Dom. I've got no one else to talk to about this. Don't fuck around with me. And don't play games. I'm in serious trouble. And I need your help."

Dom puffed on a little cigar, brushing the last stream of smoke away from Adam's face with the back of his hand. "You want my help, you got it. You know that. If you need money, whatever I've got, you've got. If you need my time, it's yours. Just tell me how I can help." Dom realized that his friend was in deeper trouble than a simple case of middle-age depression or career dead end, or any of those conventional afflictions that attack men in their forties when they realize they are not going to conquer the world, or for that matter even make a noticeable dent in it.

Adam spoke softly, anxious that no one should overhear him. "Either someone is trying to drive me crazy," he said, "or I am, in fact, crazy already. I don't know which." Adam took a hard, long drag on a cigarette and whooshed the smoke out in a fast, thin stream to underline his frustration.

Dom spoke rapidly. "You don't look crazy to me. Tired, maybe. Uptight. But from what I can see, it looks like there's a five-hundred-ton weight you want to get off your chest. So get it off. I'm not going to laugh or think you a fool." Dom puffed on his little cigar. "Maybe you forgot I spent three weeks in a psycho ward when I was in the army. Believe me, Adam, you're not the Lone Ranger; I know what it is to be stretched out as far as you can go."

Adam felt a tight soreness in his puffed-up fingers as he wrapped them around the cooling comfort of his glass.

"You remember that night at my house about a month or so ago when someone threw those cats through my window at four in the morning?"

Dom nodded. "You told me about it on the phone. That's not the kind of night one forgets. But, then, it's not the kind of night one attaches too much importance to, either. Some drunk or psycho happened to pick your house out to get his jollies off. Really. I think it's that simple." The Zapata mustache disappeared behind the rim of a glass that was dwarfed by Dom's heavy, hairy hand.

"The only thing is," said Adam, "things like that have happened to me since then. A number of times."

"For instance?"

"For instance, last night I opened up my refrigerator to get a cold beer, and the entire refrigerator was filled with dead frogs. Baby frogs. Dozens of them. Maybe hundreds. I swear the biggest one was smaller than the tip of your little finger. They must have only been a day or so-old. Maybe a few hours. Anyway, they were scattered all over the refrigerator. In the butter dish. In milk cartons. I had to throw everything out."

Dom was silent. He stared at Adam. Adam continued, his voice a whisper of remembered fear: "Frogs. Cats. Baby birds crushed in their nest and put under my bed sheets. I don't know what's coming next. And the phone calls . . ."

Dom couldn't wait. "For Christ's sake, man, why haven't you called the police? Some madman is doing the sickest number I ever heard of right in your house. And you sit here telling me about it. I'd be on the fuckin' phone to the cops so fast you . . . but wait a second . . . wait a second. What'd you start to say about the phone calls?"

Adam sipped his second martini. "They come every night. Or I should say, every morning. Generally after midnight. In fact, I got one the same night you were over my house the last time. The night the lights went out. Remember? I was on the phone when you left. Just before the cats came through the window. It was him."

Dom's eyes narrowed. "Him? Who's him? You know who's doing this to you?"

Adam sighed, sipped his martini, and shook his

head slowly. "I don't know who he is. But I do know this. I know who he thinks he is." Adam stared straight and hard at Dom. "He thinks he's my son."

Dom leaned forward, closer to Adam. "You've never had any children, have you?"

"No. I know that I haven't," said Adam. "You know that I don't have any. But whoever's calling me doesn't know that. He says that his name is Robert. And that he's my son. Some nights when he calls, it's the voice of a baby. Then the next night the voice of a young man. Some nights, a child or a teenager. He even went so far as to place a person-to-person call to me from Tampa, collect."

Dom hit the bar heavily with his hand and smiled in spite of the tension that surrounded the two men like a tangible force. "The guy's not only a psycho," said Dom, trying to lighten his tone, "he's got some culones."

"I didn't accept the call," said Adam, "I just hung up on the operator. But the minute I hung up, I wished I hadn't. For some reason I can't explain, I wanted to talk to him, to hear him. The whole thing is sick."

Dom tipped his martini glass at its base and rolled its rounded edges back and forth on the bar in front of him. "The only people you should be talking to are the police. For all you know, Adam, you may be having nightly conversations with the next Charlie Manson. Why haven't you called the police?" His voice was more plaintive than curious.

The two men looked into each other's eyes; Adam lowered his gaze. When he spoke, it was the voice of a man fighting back rage and fear and frustration. Dom had heard the same kind of voice before, in Korea, when a young West Point lieutenant had quietly come apart in a bunker on the first peaceful night after six straight days and nights of suicidal assaults by the enemy.

"I know it must seem strange to you that I haven't called the police," said Adam. "I'm sure at first I must have thought about it. But not now. I don't know how to say it."

Adam was only a word or two away from tears. Dom slid his arm around Adam's shoulders. "Hold it. Hold it," he said. "There's plenty of time to get it out." He looked around. Nobody at the bar had noticed the scene.

A quick, gagging sound came from Adam's throat; he shook his head rapidly from side to side. "Oh, Christ Almighty, Dom, what's happening to me? I don't know why I haven't gone to the police. Maybe it's because I'm so ashamed."

Dom sat up stiffly. "Ashamed. What the hell have you got to be ashamed of? You haven't done anything wrong. You're just the innocent victim of a crazy out there."

Adam took a big, long swallow of his martini. He breathed deeply. "Then tell me why do I feel an enormous sense of guilt that this is happening to me? Why have I been singled out? Why would someone, anyone, pick me out? Why me? Why not you? Why not anyone else? Why me?"

Once again Dom's hand moved reassuringly across Adam's back. "It's your nerves, Adam. This whole episode would be enough to turn anyone's nerves inside out. You just can't think straight anymore. You've got to talk to the police. They can give you a lot more help than I can." Dom brought his hand down on Adam's shoulder, punctuating his remark with an age-old gesture of friendship. "I'll tell you one thing, Adam. If all that craziness were happening to me, I wouldn't sleep one night in that house without talking to the police."

Adam had regained his composure. He lit a cigarette, inhaled, and held the white smoke deep in his lungs for five or six seconds, then let it slide out slowly in a sigh that communicated his exhaustion more convincingly than any words he had spoken. "There's more, Dom. Much more. And I'd like to talk to you about it before I talk to the police or a doctor or anyone else. There's more to this than you think. More to this than I understand. Or may ever understand. But I've got to take my time and get it straight in my head and talk to someone I trust. And that's you, Dom. I trust you." Dom nodded in the semidarkness that afforded the two men a tenuous privacy. "Like, I said, Adam, if you want my time, it's yours."

"Good," said Adam, draining his martini. He placed the empty glass back on the bar with the first positive gesture he'd made since they'd started talking.

"Good," he repeated, "now let's go to lunch. I don't want you to hear how loony I am on an empty stomach."

Dom smiled, and put a ten-dollar bill down on the bar. "The drinks are on me," he said, "and the lunch is on you."

An hour later, Dom said he was glad that he'd ordered the broiled snapper. "Tender. Really excellent, and not too filling." Adam made a comment that his London broil was also very good, but the truth was that he'd barely tasted it. A pudgy waitress with teased hair, a raucous laugh, and the hands of a wide receiver made the plates disappear in a blur of professionalism. "Any dessert, honey? Coffee?" She was looking at Adam, who looked back at her, but obviously didn't see or hear her.

Adam continued his silence. "What's the matter, hon? Tie one on last night?" Dom answered for him. "No, sweetheart. It's just that my friend is in the advertising business, and right now his brain is wrapped up in some campaign that'll have all the housewives and waitresses in town buying bust development courses at their local Vic Tanny's."

The loud laugh was quick and unaffected. "Hon, that's one thing I don't have to worry about."

"Ah, yes," said Dom, "I can see that."

"I'll have coffee," said Adam. "Black."

"Good for you," said the large waitress as she balanced an assortment of dishes in front of her.

"Make that two," said Dom. "And make mine with cream and sugar."

Adam smiled blankly and watched as the waitress walked away in the direction of the kitchen. "What I'd like to do now," he said to Dom, "is talk pretty much straight through. I know a lot of it will sound like nonsense. But, please don't say anything or ask any questions until I'm finished. Let me tell it my way. Then I'll want to know what you think. And which I should see first. The police or a psychiatrist."

Dom lit a small cigar. Adam began talking.

"Have you ever experienced terror? It's not that you're afraid of what could happen to you, or what might happen to you. You're desperately afraid of what *is* happening to you. You're afraid because you don't understand it. Any of it. And you can't control it."

The waitress returned with the coffee, placed the cups in front of the two men, and left without comment.

"I think I had received one phone call from my friend, or my son, or whatever you want to call him. One phone call before the night you came over to my house after the basketball game and I went through the whole episode with the cats.

"Then, of course, there was the call on that night. When the lights went out. Nothing except a baby crying and making stupid baby talk.

"I could cope with those calls. No problem. At first I thought they might be wrong numbers. Or someone like Schiff down at work playing his sick version of a practical joke. I can't say that those calls bothered me terribly. But then, the day Martin died, it all began to go haywire. I don't know if I told you, but I was the one who discovered his body. He'd called me just a few moments earlier and asked me to step into his office. And by the time I'd stepped into his office, he was already dead. Heart attack. The little shit looked like a stuffed squirrel, I remember that. Only about thirty-eight or thirty-nine, I guess. Left a wife and two daughters."

Adam paused to light a cigarette. Dom stared down into his coffee, as if the story Adam were telling could be seen on instant replay inside the cup.

"While I was in his office getting used to the fact that I was standing in a room with a dead man, the phone rang. It kind of startled me, I guess. So I picked it up. A simple, reflex action. The voice on the phone was the voice of a young boy, maybe ten or twelve. He identified himself as Robert Reynolds. He said he wanted to speak to his father, Adam Reynolds. And then he asked me if the man in the room with me was dead."

Dom looked up from his coffee cup.

"I know," Adam continued. "How could he know I was in that office? How could he have reached me? I checked afterward; the girl at the switchboard said she hadn't received any calls for

me that afternoon, and that she certainly would
have remembered any caller who wanted to speak
to me in Mr. Martin's office—especially a young
boy. How could he have known to ask me if Martin was dead? Martin must have had the attack
only moments before I came into the office. And
it was a heart attack. The autopsy showed that. No
evidence of anything unnatural."

Dom interrupted: "Excuse me, Adam, but from
what you're saying, there's ample evidence of
something unnatural or . . ."

"Or I was hearing things and imagining things,
right?"

Dom tapped his hand softly on the table. "I
didn't say that; you did. But I will say this: I
imagine the shock of finding someone dead, when
you had spoken to that person only moments before, could unhinge your mind for a bit. I'm not
saying it did, mind you, but I think you've got to
admit that you had a hell of a shock."

"Are you a psychiatrist now, Dom?" Adam's
voice was faint, tired.

"I'm sorry, Adam. I promised not to talk, just to
listen."

Adam smiled a soft, gentle smile that seemed to
say that he understood Dom's doubts about the
phone call.

"What you really want to know is am I absolutely sure I received that phone call? That the
boy asked me if Martin was dead? Or could it be
that I imagined it? Maybe. I'm not absolutely sure
of anything anymore. But I did find this on Mar-

tin's desk right after I spoke to the boy on the phone." Adam reached into his jacket pocket and pulled out a small photograph. "Here." He handed it to Dom, who squinted, trying to focus on the small picture in the dim light of the Yorkshire Inn. Adam pushed the candle on the table closer to Dom. "Here," he said, "hold it close to the candle."

What Dom saw was a snapshot taken maybe fifteen years earlier of a little boy about six years old. He was wearing short pants. There was a dog in the pic e. And, Dom thought, a 1962 Oldsmobile. "Notice anything strange about the picture?" asked Adam. Dom studied it closely.

"Frankly, Adam, no. It looks like a nice little picture of a kid and his dog and probably the family car. What's the mystery?"

Before Adam could answer, the waitress with the teased hair appeared at the table. "Anything else, fellas? More coffee? Dessert?"

Dom smiled. "Do I look like I need dessert?" He hit his swollen stomach with his fist.

"I'll take a Hennessy and some more coffee," said Adam.

"Good idea," said Dom. "Make that two."

The waitress scribbled some hieroglyphics on the card in her hand and disappeared as quickly as she'd appeared.

"Now," asked Dom, "what's so strange about this picture?"

"I don't know that it's strange, but for some reason it bothers me. The kid. Look at his mouth. It looks like he's got a harelip. A horrible one at that."

"So," said Dom, "there are thousands of people with harelips. I still don't see the connection."

"Turn it over," said Adam.

Dom turned the snapshot over, holding it close to the candle. He read the message aloud. "Hi, Daddy. I miss you. Your son, Robert."

Dom lifted his eyes slowly from the written words and looked at Adam. "That's right, Dom. The boy's name is Robert. The name of the young boy I spoke to on the phone in Martin's office. And the same name that was on the note that was wrapped around the cat's neck that night. Remember? I told you about it. 'More of a shot than Robert got.' One more thing," said Adam. "I'm aware that there are millions of boys named Robert. I'm also aware that when I spoke to that boy on the phone, he had a strange way of speaking, a difficult time pronouncing certain words. It wasn't until a few days later that it hit me. He sounded like someone with a bad harelip."

Dom turned the snapshot back over so that he was once again looking at the face of the boy. He started to say something, then stopped. The pudgy waitress with the glacial hairdo returned with the coffee and the Hennessys in two large brandy snifters. She set them down in front of Dom and Adam.

Dom smiled politely, the kind of smile that says "We like you well enough, but please leave us

alone to discuss something important in privacy."
The waitress left without a word.

There was silence for a few seconds, except for
the weak sounds of garbled conversation coming
from the few tables which weren't deserted by
this time.

"So," said Dom. "You think there's a connection
between this photo and the phone call you received in Martin's office?" He paused, picked up
the brandy snifter, but didn't bring it to his lips.
"And," he went on, "between the photo and the
phone calls you've been receiving at your house?
Along with the cats and the frogs and the crushed
baby birds?" He stopped, and then as if he only
heard his own words well after he'd spoken them,
he added, "God, what a sick conversation this is."

"Yes," said Adam. "But then, I told you it
would be. And there's more I want to say to you
about it, so please, let me continue for a while
longer."

Dom nodded.

Adam sipped his Hennessy, grimaced slightly,
then spoke again.

"Of course," he said, "a lot of possibilities have
entered my mind. Perhaps I do have a son I don't
know of. It could have happened. You know what
I mean. The result of a one-night stand somewhere along the way. And then, as the kid grows
up, the mother gets bitter and starts using him as
her tool of revenge, pouring all kinds of vicious-
ness into the kid's head until his hatred for his father becomes all-consuming. So the kid goes off

the deep end and starts hunting down a father who doesn't even think he's ever had a son."

Dom puffed deeply on a baby cigar, then spoke with the cigar still clenched tightly between his teeth, a gold-lined tooth reflecting the candle's glow. "Sounds like something out of Hitchcock. Or maybe Kafka."

Adam nodded agreement, then continued: "So if that's the case, I'm up against a young madman who may or may not be my son. But I really don't think that's it. I've searched and searched my mind, recalling the women I've had affairs with over the years. Virtually all of them remained friends of mine after things broke up. And if they didn't remain friends, at least I'd bump into them from time to time. And I'm virtually certain that none of them bore any children of mine. In fact, I'm absolutely certain."

Both men paused for sips of Hennessy, followed by swallows of coffee.

"Now," said Adam, tapping a cigarette on the back of his hand, "that leaves the casual things. The out-of-town business trip. Vacations in Europe, South America, so on. It could have happened, I suppose. But it still wouldn't make any sense. Because why wouldn't the woman or the mother have sought me out ages ago? I don't think the person who's calling me is an illegitimate child of mine born to some woman with whom I shared a bed for a night or two ten or fifteen years ago."

"May I say something here? I don't want to interrupt, but I really think I should." Dom placed his little cigar in the ashtray and waited for Adam to honor his request.

"Go ahead," said Adam, "but I bet I know what you're going to say."

"I was going to say that for a person who claims there's a strong possibility he's losing his mind, you seem to me to be lucid and clearheaded. And I agree with your thinking."

"You agree, so far," said Adam. "You may not by the time I'm finished."

"Maybe. Maybe not."

"The second thing I thought about was that kid from your place. The kid on the basketball team. The one you said saw his father cut his mother's throat wide open. The one with the dog that strangled itself leaping out the stable window."

"You mean Harold?"

"Yeah, Harold."

"What about him?"

"Don't you remember that night—the same night we went back to my house—I told you what he said to me at the basketball game?"

"He cursed at you, didn't he? Called you an ass-hole or a prick or something like that?"

"No, that's not what he said. He called me a 'Mother Fucker.' Notice, he didn't call me a 'motherfucker.' He separated it into two distinct words. And he said it twice. And then he said, 'You Mother Fuckers are gonna get yours. And you're gonna get it soon.'"

"So?" Dom rubbed the tip of his forefinger

across the bridge of a nose that had been broken more than once.

"Look, Dom, that night the kid's lousy mouth didn't exactly make me feel too good. But I can't say I paid too much attention to it. I mean, at first I never made any connection between what he said and what's been happening to me."

"And now you think there's a connection? Adam, some of those kids out there have mouths that would destroy half of civilization."

Adam shook his head slowly from side to side, then with palm facing upward, he squeezed the stem of the brandy snifter between his index and middle finger. He drank deeply until the glass was drained. He looked about in all directions. All the tables were empty now—with the exception of two at the other end of the long room, that were situated in front of a brightly blazing artificial fireplace.

"This has been a long lunch. Do you still have time?"

"All the time you want."

"All right, Dom, it wasn't just the words that Harold said that got me thinking. It was the story you told me about him. That business about the dumb three-legged dog strangling on its own leash stuck in my mind. And then I realized all the cruelty to animals I've witnessed in my own home. The kitten and its mother. Mutilated and killed. Those frogs. And the little birds. Cardinals and sparrows and bluebirds. With their necks wrung and their wings ripped off and their bodies smashed. And then something came together in my head that I didn't even realize I had been thinking about. God knows what happened to Harold's head when he saw his father slash his mother's throat, and then his own. I don't think there's any way anyone on earth could figure out how that's going to fuck up a boy's head. There's no way. And that's when I thought that maybe, just maybe, Harold's dog didn't hop out that stable window. Maybe Harold tied that leash around the post and lifted his dog out the window and dropped him. And watched him slowly strangle to death."

"That's sick, Adam. The one thing I do know is that Harold loved that dog."

"Of course. And maybe Harold's father, in his own way, loved Harold's mother. But that didn't stop him from taking a knife and opening up her neck so she could bleed to death in front of her son. And as far as sick thoughts go, do you think there's anything healthy and normal about finding baby frogs frozen to death in your refrigerator?"

"Why you? Why would Harold take off after you?"

"Who knows? Maybe I look like his father. Maybe he heard you say that I live all alone in a big house in Coral Gables. And he has this absolute feeling of abandonment. And he just hates the hell out of me. I'm not saying any of this is true. But it could be I just want the craziness to stop. And so I want you to do something for me."

Dom's eyes communicated confusion. "What? What can I do?"

"A couple of things. First, can you check into Harold's file and find out if he was an only child? More specifically, if he was the only male child."

"I know he wasn't the only child. I remember from his file. He had a baby brother or sister. I can't remember which. All I can remember was that it was only an infant. About six months old. They put it in an institution that takes care of the real small ones."

"Oh, Jesus," said Adam. "Jesus. It's him. Can you find out the baby's name for me? Can you do that?"

"I'm sure it's in Harold's file. I'll look it up this afternoon and call you back. But why is the infant's name so important?"

"Because," said Adam slowly, "it might be a boy. And if it is, his name might be Robert. And if it is, I want you to do something else for me. I want you to have Harold completely and thoroughly examined by a couple of psychiatrists. I want you to tell them what he said to me. And what's been happening in my home. And if they say Harold is all right, I want you to find a way to transfer him to some other place that handles kids like him—but someplace far, far from here."

Dom bit the tip of a small cigar and sighed. He moved his hand across his mouth. "I'm afraid I can't do either."

"I thought you said you'd help in whatever way you could?" Adam, who had started out the afternoon completely broken in spirit, now seemed the stronger, more confident, of the two men.

"I did say that, Adam. And I meant it. But you didn't give me a chance to tell you this. You wanted me to wait until you were through. I can't do those things to Harold, because I don't know where Harold is. The day after that basketball game, he ran away from Bay Hill. No one has seen him since. I thought he was gone for good."

"Oh, Jesus, no. Do you think it's just a coincidence that he disappeared the day after I had that run-in with him and all that madness started at my house?" Adam's voice was flat, emotionless; it registered defeat rather than surprise.

"Adam, I honestly think you've added up two and two and come up with twelve. First off, if I had a nickel for every kid at Bay Hill who shocked somebody with a blast of curse words or some obscene act, I'd have enough to take us on a three-week trip to Europe."

Dom grimaced, his lips tightening downward, creating the mouth of a tragic clown.

"Look, I've had cases where women and men from the community have come out to the place to act as volunteer parents for a picnic. You know what some of our kids did? Stole the women's pocketbooks, shit in them, and left them where they were sure to be discovered."

Dom held his hands out, palms to the sky. He shook his shoulders in a philosophical gesture passed from one generation of Italians to another.

"Now any kid who shits in a woman's pocket-book is not what you'd call a model boy, but it doesn't mean he's going to start making crazy phone calls and killing animals wantonly and terrifying someone he hardly knows."

"You don't think it's Harold, then?" Adam's voice came from far away.

"I didn't say that. For Christ's sake, it could be anyone. But your theory about Harold. It's a bit far out."

"Maybe the whole thing is a bit far out, Dom. The only thing I'm sure of really is the photo of the boy. Maybe I've just imagined the rest. Or dreamed it. Maybe the frogs and the birds and the phone calls are all things that are just happening in my mind. Because I don't have them anymore, you know. I put the birds and frogs in the garbage and then threw the garbage away. And the phone calls are gone, of course. And the picture. I could have found it anywhere. And what does it mean anyway? Maybe Robert is just a creature who lives in my mind. Maybe I've made everything up. Maybe I'm losing touch. That's what you're thinking, isn't it, Dom? Maybe your old friend has flipped out?"

Dom sighed. He was weary now. The oversized features of his face took on the image of a gargoyle in the late-afternoon darkness of the restaurant.

"It's not that I don't believe you, Adam. I've known you too long to doubt your honesty. It's just that I can't understand why you haven't gone to the police yet."

"The police would ask questions and eventually they would ask me the one right question, and after they did that they would either leave me alone or see to it that I was put quietly away somewhere."

Dom hunched his large frame over the table. "And what is this one right question they would ask you, Adam?"

"They would ask me who I thought was doing all these things. Killing the cats and the birds and the frogs. And making the phone calls."

"And what would your answer be?"

"I would answer that I believed the person doing it was my son Robert."

"But Jesus Christ, Adam, you don't have any son. You don't have any children. You just told me you were sure of that."

"I know," said Adam, a silly smile spreading across his face. "That's why it's going to be so hard to catch him."

"Adam, you're not making any sense."

"I know," said Adam. "Shall we go?"

CHAPTER 9

One of the traits that made Donald Schiff Martin-Philbrick's least beloved employee was his air of superiority and his belief that whatever fad or philosophy he was currently into clearly granted him access to realms of knowledge and wisdom far beyond the ken of his co-workers.

There was a period in the mid-sixties, about six or seven months, when he pursued the enigmatic truths of Zen Buddhism with all the zeal of a true convert. "Do you know what time it is?" an innocent associate might ask. Donald Schiff's face would become a mask of eternal indifference. "It is now," he would answer. "It is always now."

During this time, Donald Schiff worked extremely hard at projecting an air of inner tranquillity; he was a sage who had passed beyond the search for truth; he had become one in spirit with the universe and he made those around him painfully aware that he, Donald Schiff, was privy to a communion with the cosmos that would forever be denied them. Fortunately for these people, Donald Schiff's passion for Zen Buddhism began

to wane about the time he started to realize that
he couldn't become a Zen master in less time than
it takes to complete an Arthur Murray dance
course.

But Zen, of course, was nothing more than a
mysterious stop on Donald Schiff's journey to
greatness. For a while he found it in pop art, but
that faded quickly before the power and glory of
LSD, speed, barbiturates, and a fast little trip to
the outer limits with heroin. Then came a siege
with conventional wisdom and vodka martinis,
followed by transcendental meditation and health
foods. In between, there was astrology and sexual
liberation, relevance and isolation, and water
beds, group encounters, and primal therapy, and
karate and always a never-ending search for that
something, that anything, that would take the
edge off the loneliness and emptiness of being
Donald Schiff. And as he moved from population
control to anti-Freud to flower children to yippies
to the Beatles to Mick Jagger to motorcycles to
plastic floors and aluminum walls, to leather jack-
ets to unisex to the occult, one thing remained
constant. With each discovery, with each new
phase of his life, Donald Schiff found himself in a
position to verify his own innate superiority and
the relative inferiority of those around him. "What
do they know," he'd reason, "they've never read
Krishnamurti?" Or, "The fools. Zen is only relevant when you've reached the point of not caring
whether or not it's relevant. It'll take them years
to learn that simple truth."

Donald Schiff was an incurable romantic in that he enjoyed an intense love-hate relationship with himself. His apartment, in a luxury condominium overlooking Biscayne Bay, reflected not only Donald Schiff's tastes, it reflected Donald Schiff. There were three Donald Schiff paintings—all self-portraits—lit and hung throughout his apartment. Each depicted the artist as a dramatically heroic figure probing into the enigmatic and abstract mysteries of the universe. In each portrait, Donald Schiff had portrayed himself in an idealized state, far more handsome and physically attractive than a mirror might reflect. Nonetheless, as his infrequent guests never failed to notice, the apartment contained an abundance of mirrors, in an abundance of sizes and shapes. And while Donald Schiff avoided the obvious cliché of the mirrored ceiling, two of his four bedroom walls were ceiling-to-floor mirrors, so that whenever he wished, Donald Schiff could study his favorite subject with exquisite intensity. Sometimes he adored what he saw, and other times what he saw in the mirror threw him into an uncontrollable rage.

It so happened that during the period when Adam Reynolds was receiving those bizarre nightly phone calls, Donald Schiff had given his life over entirely to the study of Yoga. And while one basic tenet of Yoga is to rid oneself of selfishness and egocentricity, this did not present a conflict for Donald Schiff, since he had never considered himself anything less than generous and fair-minded.

"Adam, I have noticed something rather sad about you in recent weeks. You've always been such an agreeable sort. But now you're in obvious mental torment. Have you been sleeping well?"

Adam looked across his desk and up into the gray eyes of Donald Schiff and then at the man's face. The nose was prominent, the mouth clenched. The bearing and manner were of tightly coiled tension cloaked behind a voice of casual concern.

"As a matter of fact, no. I haven't been sleeping well. Not at all. Not in weeks."

"Can I ask why?"

Adam's voice was a barren monotone and his face wore a slightly silly smile. "No, you cannot ask why. But I'll tell you anyway. My house is haunted. And a strange ghost keeps me up till dawn every day." He crushed a cigarette into a massive black ashtray. Donald Schiff's manner remained friendly. "Glad to see you've still got a bit of humor about you, Adam. But I don't think you'd have the problems that keep one awake all night, if you looked after the spiritual side of life. That's the trouble with this insane country. Everyone's chasing the almighty dollar instead of seeking the peace and harmony and the oneness of the universe."

Adam looked down at the typewritten page that rested on his desk; it contained the lyrics of a jingle he had written for a chain of convenience stores in Florida, Georgia, and Alabama. The first line read, "We've got everything for you, everything you want us to." He glanced back up at Donald Schiff.

"A lecture, I take it. This is going to be some kind of lecture on how you're living right and I'm living wrong and that's why I can't sleep nights. Jesus Christ, Don, if there's one thing that will put me to sleep, it's a horseshit lecture from you."

Donald Schiff smiled and shook his head tolerantly. "How old are you, Adam?"

"Forty-four. Why?"

"You smoke about two packs a day, don't you? Drink, too. Sometimes a lot. Sometimes more than a lot. I'd say you're probably forty pounds overweight. Nervous. Anxious. In a pressure job. Just like the rest of America these days, you're heading nowhere in a hurry. Nowhere but straight to a heart attack."

Against his will, Adam could feel himself being drawn into what he often called "Donald Schiff's spectacular theater of meaningless mental masturbation."

"Oh, come now, Don, you don't give a shit if I buy the farm the same way Martin did. You're waiting, hoping, and praying to step into my job and you know it, now, don't you?"

Without invitation, Donald Schiff sat on a wicker chair a few feet from Adam's desk, indicating that their conversation would not be concluded for quite a while.

"No, I don't want your job. I've pretty much found what I want out of life. Peace of mind. That's what I've been searching for. And that's what I've found. And that's what I'd like to help you find."

Adam was too tired to play games. "You are an absolute asshole, do you know that, Schiff? Since I first met you, God knows how long ago, you've found peace and harmony at least ten dozen times. And each time you find it, you bore the shit out of everyone and anyone who'll listen, letting them know how you've found something that we all should have. Only problem is two weeks after you've found it, you lose it. You've tried everything from jogging to Jesus and you're still as much of a foppish asshole as the stupid fuckin' day I hired you."

Adam shook his head slowly, as if to indicate all the venom pouring from his mouth wasn't really his own. Donald Schiff said nothing. He smiled the Yoga smile of love and understanding which said, in essence, that he had moved beyond the personal prison of human jealousy and rage and into the freedom of universal love.

"Wipe that shit-eating grin off your face, you faggot." The frustration of the past few weeks were now clearly dominating Adam's mood. At that particular moment, he hated and despised Donald Schiff.

"It's bad karma, that's all," said Donald Schiff.

"Bad what?"

"Karma," said Don in a gentler, more sympathetic tone than Adam had ever heard him use before. "Karma is suffering. And you are suffering because you have not yet learned that your concern for yourself, your emphasis on your own personal career, your own personal preservation, your own separateness, your so-called individuality is the inevitable source of all your grief."

"No," said Adam, lighting another cigarette, "that's not all true, Don. For one thing, I'd have to say that, more than anything, you are the source of my grief." Adam's expression indicated he was not totally displeased with his attempt at humor, but it also communicated the fact that he had grown less impatient with Donald Schiff and was willing to let the man ramble on.

"I know the pattern, Adam, believe me. I know it. Because for years I was caught up in it, too. The obsession with self. I want this. I want that. This is my house. My car. My job. Me. Me. Me. I. I. I. Only when we give up this notion of 'I' can we give up suffering. And I will tell you why."

"Go ahead. Tell me why. You're going to whether I want you to or not." Adam blew a smoke ring at the ceiling.

Donald Schiff spoke as if he were the spirit of Yoga personified. "It is selfishness that causes suffering, because it is selfishness that causes desire. And it is desire that creates the endless stream of words and ideas and thoughts and acts that constantly perpetuate streams of karma. Doesn't the pursuit of pleasure itself become like an addiction? That is why Yoga has inspired so many mil-

lions, no, not millions, but billions across the face
of the earth to accept the fact of reincarnation."

Adam spoke. "Reincarnation. Am I to understand that you're now into reincarnation? You're
really something, Schiff."

"Let me tell you how and why I got into it,
Adam. And then maybe you won't think I'm quite
the idiot you've always thought me to be."

Donald Schiff leaned forward in his seat,
placed a thin white hand on each of his knees and
began to talk to Adam in an even softer tone than
he'd been using.

"You see, Adam, all my life I've been bothered
by the injustice I've seen in the world. An untal-
ented loudmouth like Martin getting reams of
money and recognition while far more talented
and worthwhile people never seem to achieve anything. They have accidents or bad luck."

"Martin had a fatal heart attack at the age of
thirty-nine. Is that your idea of good luck?" Adam
sat back and put his feet up on the desk so that
they were practically sticking in Donald Schiff's
face.

"Forget about Martin. Perhaps I used a poor example. But you know what I mean. You've seen
and known people who've done nothing but good
in their lives. Kind to everyone. Loving. Never a
bad word or mean action. And in return for their
goodness their baby is born blind. Or they have
terrible sicknesses and suffering. And then you
compare that with people who've been mean and
selfish all their lives and you see them surrounded

with wealth and success and it makes you wonder how there could be any justice in the world."

Adam blew another smoke ring. "Well, who ever said there's justice in the world? Maybe you and some silly guru, that's who."

"Please let me continue. The Orientals view life differently than we do in the West. They believe that every thought, word, and deed has an effect and that these effects will eventually return to the person who caused them. Good will return to good. Bad will return to bad. But that sometimes these effects are delayed. In fact, sometimes they are delayed so long that a person dies before these effects can return to him."

Adam removed his feet from the desk. He sensed a sincerity in Donald's voice he had never heard before. Even his eyes seemed warmer, more open.

"When this happens—and it happens virtually all the time—the person must be born again so that he can experience over and over the effects he generated in a previous life. Or should I say previous lives? And he must repeat this process over and over again until he experiences the first realization on the path to liberation from the endless chain of rebirths."

Adam spoke in a respectful tone: "And what is that realization?"

"That realization, Adam, strange as it may seem, is weariness. A weariness with the world. A weariness with the same repetitive patterns of life.

Of desire. Of selfishness. Of the illusory nature of success and failure."

"What you are saying, then, is that getting tired of life is the secret of happiness? If that were the case, I'd be the happiest man on earth."

Donald Schiff smiled. Adam thought he could read the slightest traces of condescension in that smile. But he let Donald speak.

"No, Adam, I didn't say that getting tired of life is the secret of happiness, but I might very well say that getting tired of the search for happiness is the beginning of understanding the secret."

"Okay, Donald, I'll think about that. But let me ask you this. You're saying that if a man lives a good and noble life but gets screwed by the breaks, he's getting screwed by the breaks because of something shitty he did in a previous life?"

"That's right."

"And even though he's getting screwed right now by the breaks, the good things he's doing now will eventually return to him?"

"In this life or another."

"And the reverse applies to a bad guy. If things are going good for him in this life, he'll eventually get shit on in another life?"

"That's the crudest way I've ever heard it expressed, but essentially that's right."

"And you actually believe that?"

"Me and billions of other people across this little speck of a planet."

Adam crushed out his cigarette. "You've got to admit it's a rather strange belief."

Donald Schiff sat back in his chair and was silent for a moment while he stared at the ceiling over Adam Reynolds's head. His gaze remained fixed to the ceiling while he spoke. "How could anything be strange in a universe where there are hundreds of billions of heavenly bodies? Where we've found quasars that are ten trillion times brighter than our sun? Did you know that, Adam? Ten trillion times. And did you know that scientists have found pulsars that are made up of matter so condensed that one teaspoonful weighs as much as two hundred million elephants? Did you know that? Do you think that in a universe where one teaspoon of anything could weigh as much as two hundred million elephants anything could be strange? But then, isn't the universe strange? Isn't life itself the strangest thing there could be? Why should reincarnation be any stranger than life?"

Adam drummed his fingers slowly on his desk. "I have another question for you, Donald. You said that the good done in one life may catch up to a person in a later life and the same is true about evil."

Donald nodded slowly, gently.

Adam continued: "But what about someone who did neither good nor evil. Someone who simply existed for a while?"

"A baby?"

"Something like that."

Don Schiff put his hand to his chin. "What do you mean, something like that?"

"Okay, let's say a baby, a newborn baby. If someone did something to him, could that baby come back as another person and try to get even?"

"You mean, reincarnation for the purposes of revenge?"

"Yeah."

"No. I don't think so. Reincarnation is so that an individual can receive the effect of his actions—good or bad—from previous lives. It is not so that he can extract revenge from someone or the ancestor of someone who wronged him in previous lives. Do you understand?"

"I think I understand. But I don't think I'll ever believe."

"You seemed very serious about it there, for a moment."

Adam Reynolds rose. "Only for a moment, I'm afraid. You see, Donald, I don't believe in the hereafter. Or life after death. Or people leading dozens of lives. I believe you get one shot in life. One, and that's it. And if you blow it, tough titty. Now, I've got to run. See you in the morning. But I'll tell you something, Donald, I really enjoyed this conversation on Yoga and reincarnation. It really made me think."

And with that, Adam Reynolds stepped quickly from behind his desk, stepped through the doorway, and was gone, leaving Donald Schiff alone in the office to stare at the blank white ceiling and wonder why he was ever born.

CHAPTER 10

The wind was a wild child, tossing tons of confetti on the frozen parade of parked cars that lined the street beneath Martin Kiernam's apartment.

The doctor poured himself another inch or so of brandy, sipped it slowly, and looked out the window to study great gusts of snow attacking the streetlights. Three stars, he thought. Maybe even four.

If the snow continued like this through the night, he was certain his lecture for the following day would be canceled. And that saddened him, because if there was one thing Martin Kiernam loved, it was to perform for an audience. He knew that whenever he spoke, wherever he spoke, his reputation preceded him. He was a psychiatrist, yes. But he was a dramatist and actor of the first rank also. He turned what would otherwise be dry, pedestrian lectures filled with obscure medical terminology into tense little theatrical events by assuming the various roles of the patients and doctors he described. They became, so to speak, his repertory company, and he was certain that even Shakespeare could not have created characters more fascinating than the ones in his cast. "He is," said one not unjealous colleague, "a first-rate Hamlet and a half-assed psychiatrist."

The remark eventually reached Martin Kiernam's ears and he was neither so pompous nor so dull as not to perceive the humor in the statement, and even a shred of truth.

One day, he thought, I would really like to write an epic play featuring a dozen or so of my favorite patients over the past five years.

Of course, there would have to be a part in it for Mother. She was never a patient, but she certainly meets all the other requirements.

Martin Kiernam moved away from the window, carrying his brandy with him, and settled into an ugly black easy chair. Next to the chair was a small black coffee table and on the table a thick, manuscript-like portfolio that contained the files on a number of patients whom Martin Kiernam was currently attending. He reached over to the coffee table, picked up the portfolio, then thumbed through the files till he came to the one on the redheaded woman about whom he had planned to lecture tomorrow. The brandy had made him warm and comfortable and a bit drowsy. As he glanced through her file, Martin Kiernam began gradually to drift away into the lecture hall where row after row of student interns sat spellbound by his dramatic recital of the events that had led the pathetic, silent woman to this godforsaken asylum for broken minds.

* * *

"Whether or not this woman ever speaks again or functions like anything remotely resembling a normal human being again is a question neither you nor I nor she can answer at this time. Most indicators at this time are negative. But at least we can examine and make judgments about some of the factors that sent her here in the first place. And perhaps as we understand them, we can use the knowledge we've gained to help future patients.

"The simple fact is that she was a fragile, guilt-ridden individual practically from the moment of her birth. But she functioned well enough for a number of years. Then came the disfiguring sickness. Then the abortion. And finally the desperate act of self-destruction. Now. We all know that abortion is a common, everyday fact of life these days. Millions of women across America— housewives, teenagers, executives, doctors, psychiatrists, cheerleaders, even nuns—have them all the time. In most cases, we find little, if any, permanent emotional or psychological damage. In some cases—let's say someone from a strong, conventional religious background or someone who really desperately wanted a baby but had to have it aborted for medical reasons—in some cases like these, there is emotional shock. And in cases like these, there is a definite need for psychological counseling. But in most cases, it's just a matter of time before the patient makes a complete recovery."

Martin Kiernam paused, adjusted his glasses, cleared his throat, and looked out at his audience. "In any event, I have no desire to get involved in any moral judgments on whether abortion is right or wrong, or when the fetus has rights, or whether the Federal government should subsidize abortions for the poor, or whatever. I'll leave those areas to the priests and philosophers and journalists and the Supreme Court.

"I simply want us—as human beings and as doctors—to take a long, hard look at what effects abortions may have on the mental health of some people, like our patient here. Again, we are looking at the medical and emotional aspects, not the moral.

"As you know, many, many psychiatrists—myself included—recommend therapeutic abortions in cases where we feel the woman in question—or the family—cannot adequately cope with the emotional or economic responsibility of having another child."

His tone became less authoritative, more personal.

"It's generally been recognized that giving birth to an unwanted child can have devastating psychological effects on the mother, not to mention the rest of the family. But what about the flip side of the coin? How much do we know about the psychological effects of abortion on women who do go ahead and have them, especially those who go ahead and have them with reservations or mixed emotions, or as in the case of our patient here, with great reluctance and guilt? How many of them have severe psychological reactions years later, without anyone knowing why, without anyone being able to trace them directly to the traumatic experience and emotionally repressed effects of an abortion years earlier? Here we have a patient whose mental breakdown seems directly related to her abortion. What can we learn from her that might help us with other patients? How do you react to her? How do we get her to react to us?"

Martin Kiernam smiled at his students. This was one of the things he liked best about his lectures—the audience participation. It was a shopworn cliché, but true, nonetheless. He *did* learn from his students. There were a few seconds of silence while the students turned and looked to see if any of them had raised their hands. One had. A small, balding man of about thirty-five, seated in the far seat on the left aisle, three rows from the rear of the auditorium. Martin Kiernam pointed toward him. "Go ahead."

The man rose. His voice, by the time it reached Martin Kiernam, was weak enough to sound as though it came from another room. "Not being a woman, I don't think I will ever be able to appreciate fully the enormously painful emotional conflict the patient experienced. On the one hand, she knew how horribly disfigured she herself had become, and what it was doing to her husband to know that they might become the parents of a terribly deformed child. Then, on the other hand, she wanted that baby very much. From the notes we received on the case, I see that she had even gone so far as to decide on a name. Robert, if it were a boy. Susan, for a girl."

The balding man paused, pressed a knuckle nervously against the side of his nose, then spoke again. "That brings up an interesting point. Suppose, if we could determine the sex of the fetus by, say, the eighth week of pregnancy, that the state then required that the fetus be given an appropriate name. Wouldn't that have a great effect on the rate of abortions, even today? Our patient had named her fetus. So for her, at least in her mind, the fetus was already a child. We can only imagine how she fantasized about playing with her baby. About holding it, feeding it, loving it. And then, under extreme pressure from her husband, and upon the advice of the authorities, and finally, fearing for her own life, she consented to destroy it."

"Excuse me, please. I've got to interrupt here for a moment." It was Martin Kiernam rising to his feet. "We are all indeed aware that this woman was probably torn apart—absolutely crushed and destroyed mentally because of society's and her own feelings of guilt about abortion at the time. After all, it happened more than twenty years ago. And even though abortion is still a highly charged emotional subject today in this country, now it is at least out in the open. Twenty years ago, it was criminal. Today it's merely controversial. We all understand that. But what is your point?"

"My point, Doctor, is simply that for most of us

abortion has become an abstraction, a matter of debate. For her, it was quite literally a matter of life and death, of killing her own child."

"Yes," Dr. Kiernam said, a slight tone of tension in his voice, "where is this all leading us?"

"I would think, Doctor," the balding man answered, "it must lead us directly back to the abortion itself. If we could recreate the actual scene itself, the horror of reenactment might force a crack in her catatonic shield."

Dr. Kiernam answered: "Your thinking has some merit, I believe, but I think you must realize that it would be more important to recreate the emotional atmosphere surrounding the abortion, rather than the abortion itself. The physical illness. The shame. The guilt. The pressure of it. Under proper medical supervision it's really quite a simple procedure as I understand it, and her abortion was medically supervised."

"Doctor, may I say something here?" It was the voice of an attractive, well-groomed woman perhaps thirty to thirty-five years old. She was standing in the middle of the lecture hall about three rows from the rear.

"Yes, Doctor, go ahead."

"I think, to this point, assumptions have been made about this patient that are totally unscientific and most probably wrong."

The woman brushed a wisp of honey-colored hair away from her forehead and continued:

"First off, because the patient had an abortion a few months before becoming totally catatonic is no reason at all to assume that there is a direct relationship. Maybe she fell down a flight of stairs a few months before she closed out the world. But I haven't heard anyone mention that possibility. Or maybe she had been heading toward a catatonic state since she was seven years old—whether or not she ever had an abortion. But I haven't heard any discussion of that possibility. Why is it that this woman's decision to have an abortion has been so romanticized and dramatized as if it were the only event in her life? My God, Doctor, every day thousands of women have abortions and are none the worse for it. And even those who do experience some emotional difficulty, get over it without losing their minds and becoming catatonic."

It was evident in the woman's tone of voice that she had not been pleased with the direction the lecture discussion was taking prior to her remarks.

"It seems to me we have made abortion the villain in this patient's case. Abortion and women. And I do not believe that is fair. In all probability, the seeds for her breakdown were planted long before the abortion. Had the child been born deformed or grossly defective, chances are that would have destroyed the woman's ability to function anyway. The results would have been the same. Her problems probably lie much deeper. I think we're looking in the wrong place. And as long as we insist on doing that, I don't believe we can help her."

During the woman's final remarks, Dr. Martin

Kiernam stood quietly at the podium. He looked out over the audience and directly at the woman.

"Are you finished, Doctor?" Martin Kiernam's voice showed no emotion. Only cool control.

The woman nodded mutely and sat down.

Martin Kiernam glanced at his watch, then began to address the audience.

"I regret," he said, "that there may have been a distinct failure on my part to communicate clearly. The last speaker pointed out that I had probably overemphasized the importance of the abortion in our patient's life. And then she went on to point out how society—rightly or wrongly—has made women feel such an enormous sense of guilt regarding abortion, while men have remained virtually free from this sense of responsibility. But that is exactly my point. That it was the woman herself who overemphasized the significance of the abortion until it became the dominant factor in her life. This woman grew up thirty-five years ago. And she had her abortion in a different world from the one we live in today. I think the abortion in her case was a devastating blow to an already fragile mind.

"Now, how can we . . ."

"Ooowoowoo." It was the wail of a sick, frightened animal mixed with the cry of a desperate human being on the far side of hope. It hit Martin Kiernam's ears with such sudden fury that for a full second or two he lost all sense of time and place and wondered whether he, too, had not lost his mind.

"Ooowoowoowo." It echoed across the auditorium and Martin Kiernam could see the stunned looks of disbelief and disorientation across the faces of students in the first few rows.

"Ooowoowoowoo." The gaunt, ghostlike, redheaded woman in white was on her feet now, screaming and bellowing and roaring. She turned, still howling with all the horror of a Hiroshima survivor suddenly realizing what had happened—and faced Martin Kiernam. For a moment the doctor felt faint, clutching at the podium as the woman stared wildly and blindly into his eyes and howled, "Oowoowoowo."

After a few seconds that scarred Martin Kiernam's mind with a kind of terror he had never known before, he saw some students from the first row of the audience—two men and a woman—trying to hold and quiet the redheaded patient whose screams grew louder, fiercer, more frantic. As one male student reached to grab her shoulder, her head pivoted sharply and savage teeth clamped down on the student's index finger. His scream of agony replaced hers and he fought, along with the other students, to remove his finger from the vicious, sharklike mouth that chewed and gnawed voraciously. Martin Kiernam stood frozen and silent at the podium, his hands clenching its sides as if only by clinging to it could he cling to sanity, cling to life.

Blood spilled out of the mouth of the redheaded woman as the two struggling students finally wrenched the torn finger from her mouth. Only it wasn't a finger anymore. The entire portion closest to the distal joint was gone. What remained was a raw stump spewing blood all over. The student whose finger had been severed screamed louder than ever at the awareness of his loss. He began to choke and vomit. The other two students, and doctors, stunned by the gruesome sight of ripped, ragged, bloody flesh, loosened their grip on the redheaded patient, and she broke loose from them, tearing her plain white hospital gown to the waist, revealing an incredibly white and emaciated torso and two jagged scars where once she had had breasts.

She started to come at Martin Kiernam, and he could see her still chewing on the remains of the finger in her mouth. She stopped moving forward, swallowed painfully, and dropped to the floor, holding her sides as if she had just taken poison. Martin Kiernam was still unable to move from the podium. Student doctors poured onto the stage, some of them surrounding the colleague who had lost part of his finger, yelling out, "Tourniquet. Apply a tourniquet," and "Get the rest of his finger out of her mouth. Get it out and we can sew it back on." Other student doctors flocked around the redheaded woman who was now writhing on the floor of the stage, again howling that awful sound that seemed to come from hell. "Ooowoo-woowo." The balding student doctor was the first person to reach Martin Kiernam at the podium. "Are you all right, Doctor?" There was no answer, no look of recognition in Martin Kiernam's eyes.

"Are you all right, Doctor?" Martin Kiernam blinked, then focused his eyes on the other doctor. He nodded slowly, silently.

"It's not in her mouth. She swallowed the goddamned thing," screamed one frantic voice. "Stay back," warned another.

"My finger. My finger. She's got my finger." There was agony and outrage in the voice of the student doctor who'd had the misfortune to put his hand near the redheaded woman's mouth.

"Quick, quick, get him over to surgery before he loses any more blood."

"Ooowoowoo."

"Get the fucking finger. It's in her mouth."

"She swallowed it."

"Do something. Do something. Get something to knock her out."

A small group of five or six student doctors rushed from the auditorium, taking with them the man who had lost half his index finger, a bloody handkerchief wrapped around his entire right hand.

"Hold on. Hold on. Stand back. Stand back." It was Martin Kiernam speaking. He had regained his sense of reality and was prepared to take command of the situation. "Stand back, please. Let me through to her."

Some of the student doctors surrounding the hysterical, redheaded woman who lay writhing on the floor quickly stepped back to create a pathway for Martin Kiernam. He approached the woman slowly, cautiously. He realized that every student doctor was watching him intently and he didn't have the vaguest idea about what to do or say.

Then he was standing directly above the woman, perhaps two feet away, staring down into the birdlike emptiness of her eyes. She was clutching her abdomen and howling, "Ooowoowooo." That's when Dr. Martin Kiernam heard a voice in back of him say, "My God. She looks like she's in labor."

He could see her clearly. She *was* in labor. The contractions were coming every few seconds. She was grunting, straining for delivery. How could this be? The woman wasn't pregnant. He had seen her naked only days before and her stomach was flat, even hollow. But now the remains of the free-flowing white inmate's gown that covered her body from the waist down actually seemed to swell into a mound. And her hands clutched at the mound as if she were trying to help it move out of her body.

"Stand back, please. Give her room to breathe." Martin Kiernam knelt beside the woman and gently touched her forehead. "It's going to be all right," he said. "Everything's going to be all right."

Her eyes slowly changed from inhuman marbles set deep in their sockets, into confused, lost, searching human eyes that sought out Martin Kiernam's. And then the woman spoke. "My baby," she said, her voice weak, gentle, pleading, "don't let anything happen to my baby. Please don't let anything happen to my baby."

Martin Kiernam continued to stroke the women's brow. She was sweating furiously, and with the sudden spasms of pain wracking her body at regular intervals, it was evident that she was, indeed, in labor.

Martin Kiernam did not want to do anything to startle the woman and send her back into the solitary confinement of a catatonic state. "Nothing's going to happen to your baby. Everything's going to be fine. Trust me."

He wanted very much to touch the white mound rising beneath her inmate's gown, but feared to make any sudden gesture without her knowledge and approval. "Listen," he said, his voice sympathetic, "I want to help you. I want to help you have your baby. May I?"

"Please don't hurt my baby," she said. "I've suffered so much to have him. Please don't hurt him."

She is, thought Martin Kiernam, the most pathetically defenseless creature I have ever seen. And yet a few moments ago she chewed off a man's finger. To and through the bone.

He continued stroking her brow. "I promise I won't hurt your baby. I wouldn't hurt him for anything in the world. I just want to help. Please, may I touch him gently? I just want to feel to see if he'll be delivered headfirst. I just want to feel to make sure everything is all right."

The woman's face contorted in pain for a few seconds. Then it relaxed. She stared up at Martin

Kiernam. "All right," she said, "but please don't hurt him."

Very, very slowly, Martin Kiernam lifted his hand from the woman's brow. He held it above her face so she could see it clearly, then moved it slowly down over her body without making contact. It came to rest a few inches above the white mound of her stomach. Gently, gently, he brought his hand to rest on the mound, only to feel it collapse like a balloon oozing out air, and he was suddenly touching the sharp bone of her pelvis.

"Ooowoowoo." The cry was more horrible and painful than before. The redheaded woman sat upright quickly, her hands at Martin Kiernam's ears, her fingers stabbing at his eyes. And she screamed, "What have you done to my baby? You've killed my baby. Where is my baby? Where have you taken him?"

Martin Kiernam felt the woman's hands ripping and tearing at his face. Fear rose up in his throat, and he gagged on his own cry for help as the student doctors began to pull the woman away from him. Then he was free of her. He reached up and touched his face. It was covered with blood.

"Ooowooowoo."

The wind was howling harder, coughing great sheets of frozen silver across the deep, dark New York night. "Oowooowo." The ancient little Volkswagen with a broken heaten became a prehistoric mammal preserved in a layer of glacial ice that had somehow been deposited on a lonely street, shivering in silence beneath the window of Martin Kiernam's apartment. The man looking down from that window drank slowly from the brandy snifter he held in both hands. Four stars, he thought, this is going to be a four-star storm.

He had grown tired of playing the game he always played—imagining his lectures erupting into incredible displays of pyschodrama. Surely tomorrow's lecture, if it wasn't called off because of the snowstorm, would be as dry and repetitious and routine as most lectures. His students wouldn't engage in heated debates; half of them would be interested in what he had to say, the other half would stare at the podium with eyes glazed over with monumental indifference. The redheaded woman wouldn't rise to her feet, screaming and roaring with unborn rage. She wouldn't bite off a student doctor's finger. Martin Kiernam wouldn't freeze in a state of shock. The woman wouldn't go into false labor. She wouldn't tear at Martin Kiernam's face. Instead, she would sit in her chair, mute and motionless as she had done for years. He would make some rather obvious comments. The students would take notes. And that would be it.

Nothing would happen. Nothing ever happened. And that was Martin Kiernam's biggest trouble. No matter how hard he hoped for and imagined great tragic scenes and sudden miraculous cures, they never took place. Or rather they only took place in books and movies. In real life, everything was routine. And the incredible part was that he had gotten completely used to so much pain and humiliation and sickness. It had simply become routine. "Obscene routine," he called it. The great, sprawling wards. The constant odor of urine seemingly everywhere. Feces sprawled across walls and crammed into corners. Rotting skin peeling away, bodies that long ago ceased to resemble anything living. Festering ulcers, bleeding bedsores, the rasping wheeze of lungs frantically forcing in air. Blank faces, empty eyes, silent lips sealed shut. Forever. All in another day's work. All something that one got accustomed to in time.

And what about the inmates who hadn't become walking vegetables? What about those who didn't stand around staring into space and dumbly follow orders? What about those who retained some vestige of humanity, some semblance of individuality? Actually, Martin Kiernam had become aware, those relatively few "troublemakers" were the only people present who held the potential for breaking the god-awful routine. And the security people did not look fondly on that possibility. So, in addition to pumping them full of chloral hydrate whenever "the crazies" got a bit rammy or uppity, the security people had a plan which never ceased to amaze Martin Kiernam with both its simplicity and its effectiveness. All they did was gather the most visible and vocal "troublemakers" together in one compact group, place them all in a single ward, and have them remove their clothing, all of it.

When Martin Kiernam first visited the naked

ward, he was shocked and distressed by what he saw. Dozens upon dozens of men of all ages and sizes and colors and shapes, milling around completely naked. They looked, thought Martin Kiernam, not so much like a group of human beings plagued by severe emotional and psychological problems, but rather like a docile herd of animals mindlessly intermingling and nervously seeking the natural boundaries of their immediate surroundings. Martin Kiernam objected strenuously at first. He couldn't fathom what could be gained by treating sick human beings in such a manner. Perhaps they were "troublemakers." But they were not violent or dangerous to anyone, including themselves. All the violent inmates were kept under maximum security guard in another building. Martin Kiernam demanded an explanation of why these people were treated in this manner. And he received an explanation.

"Quite frankly," said the security head of the institution, "it is not the kindest or most professional or even most civilized way to handle them. But unfortunately it is the most efficient and the most economical. I assure you, Dr. Kiernam, that this is not Buchenwald or Auschwitz. And I am not unaware of their suffering. I truly wish I could alleviate it. But the harsh, cold facts are that we have to maintain a sense of order and discipline here. And we have to do it with a severely limited and overworked staff. And on a budget that's half of what it should be. So what I try to do is head trouble off at the pass. By grouping the

potential troublemakers together, we isolate them
from the better adjusted inmates in our care, and
thus prevent disruptive behavior from spreading.
Further, by stripping the problem inmates of their
clothing, we also strip them of much of their ag-
gressiveness. Of course, this isn't always the case.
Some of them are so far gone they don't even realize that they're naked. But overall it works. It's
not my favorite technique. I wish there were a
better way. I really do. But the important thing is
that it works and it helps us do a better overall
job."

Martin Kiernam wasn't fully satisfied with the
security chief's analysis, but in time he came to accept it. Just as, in time, he came to accept virtually everything about the place. Occasionally,
though, after a weekend trip to New York City or
a two-week vacation in the Bahamas, Martin Kiernam would experience a kind of cultural shock
when he returned to his place of residence and
work. It was, he often thought, probably not too
dissimilar a feeling from that experienced by sol-
diers who one day were guzzling gin and laughing
in the bordellos of Hawaii or Hong Kong, only to
find themselves a few days later caught up in a
maze of bullets and shrapnel and swamp rot and
the constant presence of death in the jungles of
Vietnam. The reaction was perhaps a temporary
loss of sanity. "Who am I? What am I doing
here?" On the other hand, Martin Kiernam
thought, perhaps it is a temporary attack of true
sanity. Perhaps I've grown a bit crazy myself, con-

stantly surrounded by insanity and indifference to human suffering. Perhaps it is simply my instinct for survival telling me to get my ass out of here before I wake up one day and find myself walking around naked in a ward with a couple of hundred other loonies. It could happen, you know. You've seen it happen to others. Good, competent, hardworking psychiatrists with a realistic understanding of the limits of human beings' ability to withstand emotional stress. One day you have lunch with one of them in the cafeteria and the next day he's a suicide or a full-fledged member of the funny farm. Be careful, Martin. Don't let them get you, too. Make sure the obscene routine doesn't make you so numb you're not quite sure of what you feel, or who you are or what you're doing. So hang in there, old boy. Or get the hell out. But whatever you do, don't go anywhere tonight. It's too fucking cold out. And before you know it, this entire place is going to be buried under six hundred feet of snow.

The Volkswagen was hardly visible now, a sleeping polar bear curled up on a long, narrow, glacial field of white. Martin Kiernam moved away from the window. He had seen enough to convince him that the lecture tomorrow would almost certainly be called off. Perhaps he would treat himself to a night of downing Hennessys while watching television until Johnny Carson, the late, late movie, the religious sermon, and "The Star-Spangled Banner" all merged into one glorious test pattern that stared back at him with the same blank, mindless madness as some of his patients, the redheaded woman in particular. The *TV Guide*, he remembered, was lying on the bedroom floor, deposited there the previous night, along with a psychiatric journal, a four-month-old issue of *Penthouse*, and *The New York Times Book Review* section. Might as well see if there's anything worthwhile on the tube, he thought, as he made his way across a living room cluttered with socks, unwashed underwear, and decaying bits of evidence that it was indeed a bachelor's residence.

When he opened the bedroom door, he saw her immediately, her frail silhouette framed by the light from a streetlamp pouring in through the open window directly behind her. Faint flurries of powdery snow flew around her head and shoulders. He could not see her face or her hair or any of her features clearly, but he knew it was she. He did not move. Nor did she. And then, as his eyes became accustomed to the darkness of the bedroom, he could see that she was naked.

Outside, the wind was a wounded dog. Inside, there was only silence except for the sound of her painful breathing. He saw a sudden glint of sharp light reflected from her hand and then it disappeared and then he saw it again for an instant flashing above him and then descending quickly and he felt the light moving along his neck like a laser and there was a warm, sweet rush of blood and he knew he was going to die, but he wasn't quite sure whether he was awake or dreaming.

He fell to the floor, choking on his own blood. His face rested for a moment on her cold, naked feet. Martin Kiernam managed to raise his head to look up at his executioner in a final, silent plea for mercy. And then he saw something—or thought he saw something—that made him certain that he must be dreaming. It was there, right above him, barely visible in the pale blue light of the bedroom, protruding from her pubic area. It was a penis. The crazy woman had grown a penis. Thank God, he thought, it has to be a dream, a nightmare. And he was so relieved he wanted to laugh. But he didn't. He didn't laugh. Instead, he lowered his head and let his face again come to rest on her naked feet. And then he closed his eyes. And then he died.

CHAPTER 11

The hot, rain-drenched days and nights of September had gradually drifted into the clean, cooler air of October, then November. Adam Reynolds felt the dense pressure of a South Florida summer slowly disappear. His sinuses cleared. The puffiness in his fingers, toes, ankles, and hands gradually subsided. And the phone calls stopped. That was the most important thing. The phone calls stopped. Adam couldn't recall exactly when he'd received the last one, or if there was a pattern to the way they'd gradually diminished in frequency from every night, to three or four times a week, to once a week, to none a week. The first night that he didn't receive a phone call, of course, was something of an event. The calls had become so much a part of Adam's life that he was actually a bit unnerved when he waited all through the night and through the first hours of dawn and early-morning sunshine without the phone ringing once. It was, Adam recalled, a night on which he became intimately acquainted with the awesome power of silence to permeate a given space and make him feel imprisoned by the absence of any noise except the occasional croaking of a frog or the heavy hum of a jet gliding through a sea of darkness directly overhead.

When he realized that the hour had reached four o'clock in the morning and no one had called, Adam began to wonder why. Perhaps something had happened to his caller. Maybe he'd been in a car accident or suddenly taken sick. Perhaps his caller had gotten drunk, or run off to another town, or perhaps found another person he preferred to drive insane. Adam was amused by the way he referred to the caller in his mind as "my caller"—as if there were somehow a bond that united them in a secret, special way. Could it be that Adam was actually getting jealous, imagining "my caller" leaving Adam waiting for the phone to ring while "my caller" busied himself with newer, fresher, more inspired nighttime phone conversations? Adam wondered if "my caller" did indeed phone other people. And if he did, was the routine the same? Did he pretend to be a baby? Or a teenager? Perhaps he was entirely different with each person he called. With one, he might be frankly obscene. With another, harsh and angry and threatening. Perhaps with Adam, he'd just decided to be mysterious. In any event, Adam spent the long, lonely hours stretching from midnight to the delivery of the morning milk at 8:15 A.M. in an anxious and strangely confused state. On the one hand, he fervently hoped the phone calls would stop forever and leave him in peace. And yet, at a different level of consciousness, Adam realized that even though the phone calls were destroying his life, they were the only thing of any significance that had happened to him in years, the only adventures that lifted his life out of the endless monotony of moving through an empty and incredibly boring middle age. True, the phone calls made Adam Reynolds feel a monstrous sense of fear and impending doom. And he hated them. And yet, in a way that he could never have explained even to himself, he welcomed them. The phone calls made him feel fear. And that feeling of fear made Adam Reynolds realize that he was alive, which was something he hadn't realized very often in recent years.

When he was fully sure that there would be no phone call that morning, he showered, shaved, got dressed, and went directly to work without any sleep or any breakfast. Nervous energy kept him going through the day. After work, he returned home immediately and sat down to wait for the phone call.

He awoke at 9:15 in the morning, still dressed in his clothes from the previous day, still seated in the same chair on the back porch he had been seated in since nightfall. He rubbed the sleep out of his eyes and stared at a red cardinal perched on the edge of a branch that dipped precariously over the water in the swimming pool. When he realized that another night had passed without a phone call, Adam Reynolds rose from his chair, stripped off his stale, sweat-soaked clothes, and stood naked in the privacy of his porch. Then he opened the screen door and walked out to the pool whose surface was covered with seeds and leaves that had fallen from the massive poinsettia that stood poised like a giant umbrella shielding the backyard from the burning Florida sun. He descended the steps into the pool, feeling the cool water rise up to swirl about his feet and legs and finally, deliciously, up around his testicles. Then he dove into the water, slicing beneath the sea of leaves and seeds, swimming down into the outer-space silence at the bottom of the pool. He rested there for a moment, squatting on the floor of the pool with his legs braced beneath him, and held his breath for as long as he could. Then he pushed off the floor of the pool with all the power his legs could summon and he soared through the water like a missile climbing through the atmosphere. When he broke the surface of the water, he was laughing harder than he had laughed in years. He did not go to work that day. He stayed in the pool and laughed and played in the water by himself for hours. Later, he got dressed and went to the Ranch House Restaurant and ordered an enormous breakfast of steak, eggs, home fries, toast, and coffee which he ate with great vigor and enjoyment. That afternoon, he went to see a Peter Sellers movie and laughed himself silly. In the evening, he called a divorced woman of thirty who had worked at his office the previous year. He took her to cocktails, then dinner, then home to her bed where the two of them made love for

the first time as if they had known each other's
bodies intimately for years. Then he got dressed,
returned home, got undressed, and jumped naked
into his bed where the cool sheets and soft hum of
the room air conditioner put him quickly into a
deep, peaceful, dreamless sleep. About two
twenty in the morning, the phone rang.

For a while, the break in the pattern of regular
nightly phone calls caused Adam Reynolds's emotional moods to fluctuate dramatically. No calls
for three nights and he would be nervously talka-
tive at the office. And then, the night after a call,
he would be morosely silent, speaking only when
spoken to, and even then barely uttering the few-
est works possible. But gradually the intervals between phone calls lengthened until a week passed,
then two, and finally three. The joke is over,
thought Adam. Whoever's been getting his kicks
at my expense has either had all the fun he's
wanted or he's simply gotten bored with the
whole business. Thank God.

With the phone calls at an end, Adam Reynolds
gradually returned to what those around him un-
doubtedly regarded as a more sensible attitude toward everyday living. Now that his mind was
clearer, calmer, he took logical steps to prevent
this kind of harassment in the future.

He called a security company for an analysis
and estimate of his house's security needs and
their approximate costs. And then he did something which he realized he should have done years

ago, something far more important than the mere installation of burglar alarm systems and electronic eyes. He decided to sell his house. Right after the Christmas holidays he would see a broker and put the goddamned thing up for sale. It was ridiculous anyway, a bachelor living alone in such an enormous house, so many rooms empty and lifeless all year round, so many things like the roof and the plumbing constantly needing maintenance and constantly being neglected.

When he and Louise had moved into the house years ago, all that had been required was a small down payment. Only last year the mortgage had been completely paid off. The house was his, free and clear. And with the years, its value had skyrocketed. Not only had the value of houses in Coral Gables risen continuously over the past two decades, but the value of large, older two-story Spanish-style houses had risen at a rate that far exceeded the average. There was no doubt about it. His house was now worth a small fortune. How much? Ninety thousand dollars. At least. Maybe $125,-000. Wouldn't that be something: $125,000 cash. With that kind of money, he could be a bit more independent. Maybe take a vacation for a year. Just go away and get his head straightened out and come up with some kind of idea about what to do with the rest of his life.

Up until now, it hadn't been too spectacular, he knew. It was incredible, the way the years wasted away, one decaying into the next with hardly any notice at all, until one day you wake up and there are bulging varicose veins in your leg and a lousy little sore on your chest that keeps growing larger and you can't remember the last time you felt really good about anything. Well, the hell with that. Maybe those crazy phone calls were a good thing after all. Maybe they made him wake up to the fact that he'd been letting his life slip away. Maybe now he could take his life in his hands and still make something of it. Maybe with that $125,-000 he could buy himself a little time and peace and a chance to make a new start. Why not? He needed that house like a hole in the head, he realized. And he needed that $125,000 like he needed the very air he breathed. The decision was firm.

Right after the holidays, he'd take a leave of absence or quit his job and let that asshole Schiff take over as creative director. And what a shitty job it really was, he thought. Trying to con people into buying things they don't want with money they don't have. But that was all in the past. He could feel excitement surging through him as he began to think about where he'd go first. London? He'd always wanted to go back. Rome? He'd never been there, but he could easily see himself living as a romantic expatriate, drinking wine and sharing secrets of the heart with eager young schoolteachers from the States who'd come to Italy in search of truth and beauty and wisdom.

Oddly, the first postcard he received was from Rome. It was a color photograph of St. Peter's Square at sunset. Absolutely beautiful, Adam Reynolds thought, as he turned the card and wondered who could be writing to him from Rome. "Sorry I haven't been in touch the past few weeks," it began, "but as you can see, I've been out of the country. Rome is really magnificent. The people here are so alive, so real. Hope to be back in the States for Christmas. Will call you the moment I get back. All the best. Robert. P.S. I really miss you. Hope you haven't forgotten me already."

When Adam Reynolds finished reading the card for the third time, he checked the postmark to see if it actually had been mailed from Rome. It had. He carried the card with him up to his bedroom and lay quietly on the bed, holding the card a few inches above his eyes, studying it carefully as if it held some secret information that would pour out of it if only he had enough patience. He lay there for an hour, staring at the card. Gone were all thoughts about selling the house, about quitting his job, about making a new start. After an hour, he slowly tore the card into little pieces and lay on his bed, staring at the ceiling.

The next card, four days later, came from Paris. A full-color photo of the Champs-Elysées was on one side of the card, and on the other, a typewritten message:

Paris is fabulous. And so are the prices. Took a drive through the Loire château region yesterday. Down to Tours, Poitiers, a little place called Azay-le-Rideau. Really lovely. Today, I took in Sacré Coeur, wandered around Saint-Germain-des-Prés. I love Paris, but am not too crazy about the French. Will call the minute I get back.

Robert

An hour after he had received the second postcard, Adam was on the phone to Dom Petrella.

"Adam. You must have ESP. I was going to call you just this moment." The voice was friendly, tired, and a touch nasal: a sure sign that Dom Petrella had been drinking heavily the previous night.

"Can you come by the house this afternoon, Dom? Or this evening? I've got something I want to show you. . . ."

There was silence on the line for a few seconds before Dom spoke.

"Has the phantom struck again?"

"Yes."

"Anything ugly? Any damage done?"

"No, nothing like that. I'll show you when you get here, if you're coming."

"I'm coming."

"What time?"

"Give me two, two and a half hours."

"Say about five thirty?"

"Yeah, I should be there by then."

"Okay. I'll see you then."

"Oh, by the way, Adam, I said I was going to call you anyway. It's about Harold. I've got some information on him that I'll give you when I get there. And you asked me to see if I could find out what his little brother's name was. Whether or not it was Robert. Well, I can't find out anything. Somebody got into our files and took all our records on Harold. The works. It was probably Harold. He probably took them before he ran away. Although why he'd want them beats me. Unless he just wanted to destroy them."

Adam interjected, "It makes sense."

"What makes sense?"

"That he'd want to destroy his records, destroy his past, so to speak. If someone's going to take on a new identity, become a new person, the first thing they'll try to do is destroy their past, wipe out everything that's behind them. Then you see, they can invent their own life as they go along. Even make up a new past. A new history of who they are. That way, if you don't like who you are, you can become whoever you want to be."

"Hey, Adam, the kid simply took a few pages of statistics and psychiatric records. Don't make it anything more than it is."

"Don't you realize," said Adam, "that those records were all he had in the world? The only thing that proved where he came from, who his parents were, what his family was like? With those records gone, he can become anybody."

"Well, who do you think he's going to be?"

"I don't know. Maybe he's become Robert."

Neither man spoke for the next ten seconds.

Then Dom Petrella said softly, "I'll try to get there by five."

Adam was still holding the receiver to his ear when he heard the sudden click followed by a dull dial tone. Then he placed the phone back in its cradle and walked back into the living room where he sat down and stared at the typewritten message on the card from Paris. It looked, he thought, as if it could have been typed on an IBM Selectric, just like the ones at his office. He studied each individual character in each word, hoping to find an irregularity, a distinctive flaw that somehow might help him track down the actual typewriter used for the message. But how could that help? he thought. There must be two hundred million typewriters in the world. Two hundred million typewriters. The phrase struck a chord in his mind. What was it? Oh, yes, the thing Donald Schiff had said down at the office about two hundred million elephants. What did he say exactly? And then Adam Reynolds could hear Donald Schiff's voice as clearly as if he were in the room. "Did you know that scientists have found pulsars that are made up of matter so condensed that one teaspoonful weighs as much as two hundred million elephants? Did you know that? Do you think that in a universe where one teaspoonful of anything could weigh as much as two hundred million elephants anything could be strange?"

Everything is strange, thought Adam Reynolds. And nothing is strange. And then in his mind's eye he tried to create an image of two hundred million elephants working diligently on two hundred million typewriters, their great, huge feet delicately striking exactly the right keys.

It's strange, he thought, that I received those phone calls. And then the postcards. But is it stranger than two hundred million elephants? Or stranger than my sitting here? Or even being here? And then Adam Reynolds began to wonder why he was alive and why Harold was alive. It was all so strange why anyone was alive. He remembered reading once what incredible odds there were against being. Just simply being. Hundreds of millions of sperm seeking out one minuscule egg. And of all those hundreds of millions, only one sperm would make it.

He recalled that someone had once figured that all the eggs it took to provide the world with its present population could fit into a top hat. Three billion eggs in a top hat. Now that was something to think about. That was strange. But how about the sperm needed to fertilize those eggs? All the sperm responsible for all life on the planet earth today could fit into a thimble. A thimble, for Christ's sake. So what was so strange about a teaspoonful of anything weighing more than two hundred elephants? That was nothing.

And then Adam remembered something he had heard a scientist say on television one night. "The universe," the scientist said, "is not only queerer than we imagine, it is queerer than we *can* imagine."

"No shit," said Adam Reynolds to no one in particular. "No shit."

Dom Petrella arrived at 5:15. The men exchanged halfhearted backslaps, then proceeded immediately to the back porch where they could watch the late-afternoon sun splash bright lemon streaks across the kidney-shaped pool in the backyard.

"Scotch? Gin and tonic? Beer? What are you gonna have?" Adam was already behind the carved mahogany Spanish bar set in a corner of the porch.

"You have a real cold beer?" Dom Petrella unbuttoned his collar and loosened his tie. Bristling sprouts of Brillo-like black hair seemed to shoot up from beneath his shirt and curled around his neck.

"Bud?"

"Fine."

"All right, no sense beating each other off. What have you found out about Harold?" Adam poured two inches of gin into a long, thin glass piled high with ice cubes, then followed with a quick splash of tonic.

"I found out," began Dom, "that in addition to everything else, our little Harold is a first-rate thief."

"How's that?"

Dom used the back of a hairy right hand to brush a few flecks of foam from his Zapata mustache. "Well, for one thing, when he bugged out, he left a ring of keys behind. Under his mattress. He just forgot them I guess. Anyway, I started checking around and sure enough those keys were just what I thought they were. Keys to the Coke machine. And the ice-cream machine. And even one to my secretary's desk drawer where we keep petty cash. The little bastard must have picked up a set of my keys somehow. He had duplicates made and then replaced the originals. The little fucker. All that trouble for a few bucks. And for his records."

Adam sipped his gin and tonic. "So? So what does that mean to me? The fact that Harold is a petty thief doesn't affect me one way or another."

Dom spoke again, squinting into a giant yellow ball that seemed suspended in space a few feet above the pool. "He's not a petty thief anymore, Adam. At least I don't think so. Someone fitting Harold's description forced his way into one of Mullen's Drug Stores down in Homestead the other night. In addition to getting about four thousand dollars in cash, the son of a bitch took a shitload of drugs. Estimated value about three thousand dollars. He just loaded up sacks and carted the shit away."

"Are they sure it's Harold?"

"They are now."

"How's that?"

"Simple enough. Fingerprints. They got a perfect set. You see, the police knew that one of our kids had run away. I have to notify them every time it happens. So all they did was pick up some prints off Harold's personal belongings at our place. And then matched them with some they found at the drugstore around the safe. It was

Harold, all right. The dumb kid didn't even wear gloves."

"So," said Adam, "I still don't see how this affects me, except that it backs up my theory that Harold isn't a very nice kid."

"Well, Adam, I don't know. That kid's come into more money all at once than he's ever seen in his life. My guess is that he's long gone. He probably hopped a plane or train first chance he got. I don't think we'll ever see him again. I don't think I will. I don't think anyone around here will. Harold, as they say, has split."

"What makes you so sure?"

"The other kids at Bay Hill. They said Harold was always talking about getting his hands on some money and getting as far away from me and Bay Hill just as fast as he could. They say he was always talking about Colorado, Texas, Wyoming, Arizona. Places like that."

Adam stared blankly into his gin and tonic. There was no sound on the back porch, save for the monotonous hum of the old electric ceiling fan that buzzed away directly over Dom's head.

Adam looked up from his drink. "He never spoke to those kids about Europe, did he? Paris? Rome?"

"No, not that I know of. Why?"

"Because I've been getting postcards sent from Europe. Signed by Robert. That's why I called you. I wanted to show you the one I'd received from Paris to prove I'm not crazy."

He pulled the card from his pants' pocket,

walked over to where Dom was seated, and gently placed it on the table directly in front of him. Dom studied the card silently for a moment. Then he spoke. "Well, I don't know if this will be any encouragement to you, but this card is typewritten, and there are no mistakes on it. In typing. Or in spelling. And I know this about Harold. He couldn't type. And he was the worst speller and one of the worst students we had at Bay Hill. And going to Paris is totally out of character for the kid. He could barely speak English."

Adam sipped his gin and tonic without comment.

Dom spoke again. "You said cards. In the plural. Where are the others?"

Adam reached into his other pants pocket and pulled out the dozen or so pieces that had been the card from Rome. "It's the only other card I received. It was the first one."

"May I have the pieces, please?"

Adam deposited all the pieces on the table a foot or so away from Dom, then pushed them gently in his friend's direction.

In a few moments, Dom had assembled the pieces in their proper pattern. "This one is handwritten. And that may be a big help."

Dom reached into his shirt pocket and pulled out a white piece of paper, unfolded it, and placed it on the table next to the hastily pieced together postcard. He looked first at the postcard, then at the note, then back again at the postcard. "Son of a bitch," he said after a long moment of concentration, "they don't look like they were written by the same person. This is a note written by Harold. He gave it to one of his friends the day he ran away. The handwriting on it is different from the handwriting on the postcard, except for one thing. The *t*s on both of them look almost exactly alike. But that's probably just a coincidence."

"Sure," said Adam, placing his empty glass back on the table, "what else could it be?"

Dom looked up at Adam and answered sharply, "I don't appreciate the sarcasm, Adam. And I don't know why you keep trying to twist this thing into some kind of pattern that makes Harold the villain."

"Well, who else am I going to pick on? You? Someone from my office? Who?"

Dom drained his beer and casually crushed the aluminum can in his hand. "How about you, Adam? How about making yourself the villain?"

"Me?"

"That's right, you."

"What the fuck are you talking about?"

Dom tapped the empty beer can on the table. He began talking in a lower, softer voice. "Well, since you're in such a hurry to convict Harold for something he probably hasn't done, let's apply the same standards of investigation and evidence to you that you've applied to him."

"For instance?"

"For instance, the second postcard was typed. You know how to type. Harold doesn't."

"You're a disaster as a detective, Dom. Millions of people type."

"Yes, Adam, that's right. But I also noticed the typeface used on the postcard is similar to the one you use on all the notes you've sent me. I couldn't help but notice, because I've always thought that type was excellent, extremely easy to read."

"This is hot shit, Dom. Are you really accusing me of doing all these things to myself? How could I call myself? How could I send myself postcards from Rome, from Paris? How?"

"How isn't really the important question, Adam. The important question is why?"

Adam's eyes went blank. This was Dom Petrella speaking, his lifelong friend. The one person on earth he trusted. "Dom, are you trying to tell me that I'm crazy? Don't be shy. Speak up. If that's what you think, say it."

Dom stood up at the table, moved away from his chair, then turned his back on Adam to look out across the backyard and stare into the sun. He spoke as if he were addressing someone he used to know a long time ago. "Take a look at yourself, Adam. You're not the same person you were six months ago, even two months ago. You've aged fifteen years."

Adam interrupted: "Don't you think something like this would take its toll?"

"I don't know, Adam. I honestly don't know what's been happening. Your appearance has gone to hell. You don't care how you dress. Or when you get a haircut. For God's sake, Adam, take a look at your fingernails. They're absolutely filthy. Can't you see what's happening to you? It's a wonder you still have a job."

Adam swirled the gin and tonic in his glass. "So that's it. I forgot to shave and that makes me a schizo?"

"I didn't say you were anything. All I said is that if we applied the same standards in judging you, that you apply to Harold, you'd make a much better suspect than him. After all, you're the only one who's gotten the phone calls. You're the only one who's heard mysterious voices."

"Looks like you've got it all figured out."

"No, I don't. I don't have anything figured out. You're my friend and I want to help you in any way I can. But maybe I can't help you. Maybe you need the kind of help I can't give."

"I see."

"Listen, Adam, I sincerely wanted to help you. I still do. But after the last time we met, the time we had lunch together, I was really worried for you. So I took it upon myself to spend some time with the staff psychiatrist at our place. The one who works with the kids with the most severe problems."

Adam began to pour himself another gin and tonic as if he were hardly paying attention to what Dom was saying.

"I did it for your sake, Adam. I honestly did. I didn't tell the doctor your name or anything like that. I just told him about the things that had been happening to you. I told him about the phone calls. And about the cats. And the frogs and the birds."

Adam looked up from his drink. "And?"

"He asked me questions. He asked me how old you were. What kind of a house you lived in. If you were married. Any children. That kind of thing. I told him about the trouble with Louise all those years ago. He was really interested in that. And he seemed especially concerned that you've lived so long by yourself in such a large house."

"Did you tell him it was a good investment?"

"Yes. He said it might be a good investment financially. But that emotionally and psychologically, it was a disaster."

"And you believe everything the good doctor says?"

"No, not everything." Dom turned back to face Adam. "But I know he's hit many, many things right on target with our kids. He thinks you might have problems."

Adam smiled, a wary, slightly sinister smile. "Well, thanks, Dom. You have no idea how relieved I am to find out that someone thinks I have problems. And look at the enormous amount of money you've saved me. I mean now that you and your Freudian friend have everything solved, there's nothing left for me to do but give myself up. Only who do I give myself up to? And for what?"

"Adam, I'm not accusing you of any crime. I'm not even accusing you of hearing voices or writing postcards or stuffing your refrigerator with crushed frogs. The only thing I'm accusing you of is ignorance. You don't know what's going on. You don't know if some runaway kid is out to get you, or if you're cracking up. And you've refused to call the police, which doesn't make any sense. All I'm saying is, have yourself checked. See a doctor. And see a good one. Maybe there's not a god-damned thing wrong with you, but for Christ's sake, find out. There's nothing to be ashamed of. And if something is wrong, then for Christ's sake we'll get it fixed. Do you understand? I'll help you in any way I can. Can't you understand that? I'm your friend." The heavy hands came up to cover Dom's face, and Adam wondered whether Dom might be trying to shield tears.

Adam spoke. "All right, Dom. What do you want me to do?"

"Will you see a doctor? Tomorrow?"

"That Freudian friend of yours?"

"No. He told me he thought it would be wrong for him to see you; what with him working so close to me every day, you might have a feeling your privacy was being violated."

Adam chuckled. "What have I got left to be private about?"

Dom continued talking as if he had not heard Adam's comment. "He has recommended another doctor, however. You can meet him and make up your own mind. But at least talk to him, will you?"

Adam nodded.

"You know, Adam," Dom went on, "I have a feeling everything's going to turn out fine. The mere fact that you're willing to see a doctor is a good sign. And if the problem isn't in your head, then I promise you this: I'll move in with you and I won't move out until we find out who's doing this shit to you. And when we do, I am personally going to crack his fucking head open. Fair enough?"

Dom extended his hand toward Adam.

"Fair enough, Dom. And I'll hold you to it. If there's no problem up here," he said, tapping his head, "then be prepared to move in." The two men shook hands.

The sun had slipped completely from view and the burnt orange glow of a South Florida dusk drifted across the backyard and onto the porch. Dom spoke. "The doctor's name is Perlmutter. I have his number at my office. I'll stop there on the way home and call you with it, okay? In about twenty minutes."

"Okay," said Adam, his voice subdued, reflecting the embarrassment he felt at having a lifelong friend inform him that he, Adam, might have become two persons living in one body. There was an awkward silence for a moment or so, then Dom excused himself with another promise to call back with the doctor's phone number in fifteen or twenty minutes.

When the phone rang, Adam was in his bedroom, lying quietly on the bed, trying to reconcile himself to the fact that he would be placing himself under the care of a psychiatrist. He rose to his feet, picked up the receiver, and was just getting ready to tell Dom he had had second thoughts about seeing the doctor when a voice that wasn't Dom's but that was nonetheless quite familiar to Adam whispered four words that were to ring in Adam's ears for the remainder of the night.

"Hi, Dad," the voice said softly, "I'm back."

CHAPTER 12

Instinctively, Adam knew that there would be no use running. He also knew that the insane charade that had dominated his life for the past few months would soon be coming to a close. Whoever was calling him would soon be visiting him. He didn't know how or why he knew this, but he knew it. It was more than a feeling; it was a conviction. In one way, thought Adam, it's going to be a relief to get it over with no matter what happens.

An eerie calm settled over the house, not unlike the unnatural peace that envelops an area exposed to the eye of a hurricane. And this serene state that seemed to Adam almost a physical presence encouraged him to make a number of decisions. First, he would not see the psychiatrist; there was no use lying on a couch trying to communicate with a stranger who would be certain to think him an absolute madman. Second, he would take an immediate leave of absence to straighten out "some important personal matters." There was no use trying to convince people to buy a particular brand of soap or soft drink when he couldn't even convince his own best friend, or himself, for that matter, of his own sanity. Third, he had the phone disconnected: if he was going to sit back and wait for Robert to arrive, he could at least do so in peace and quiet without that monstrous phone ringing at all hours of the night. He informed Dom of his decisions, then Donald Schiff and the people at the agency. And then he set about the task of getting both himself and his house in order for the arrival of his expected guest.

He took a long hot bath, soaking in the tub for more than an hour, and realized that Dom had been right: he had let himself fall to pieces. He couldn't recall the last time he had taken a bath, or a shower for that matter. He felt the days' and even weeks' accumulation of dirt dissolve and slip off his body. He scrubbed his fingernails furiously. He shampooed his hair, and shaved what must have been ten days' growth of beard. He brushed his teeth for a full five minutes, and when he had finished he realized that he had been living with a sickly taste in his mouth for weeks. God, how his breath must have offended people.

When he had finished in the bathroom, he walked into his bedroom. He opened his dresser drawer to take out some clean, fresh underwear. But of course there wasn't any. Weeks of dirty, shabby laundry and linen lay in a soiled gray mound at the foot of his bed. He hadn't even noticed it until now. Fortunately, toward the back of his closet, he found a clean striped pair of Dacron slacks and a fresh white tennis shirt, which he quickly slipped into without benefit of underwear. Then, not bothering to hunt for clean socks which he knew did not exist, he poured talcum into a pair of loafers and stepped easily into them. He felt like a new man. But when he studied himself in the mirror, what he saw was a clean, neat old man. Again, Dom had been right. Adam had lost about thirty-five pounds. He had needed to lose the weight, but not like this. His clothes were baggy, their very size making them seem grotesquely out of style. His skin was pale, almost gray, and loose. His eyes had moved farther back in his head. Lines were etched in his face that he had never seen before, especially around the mouth. I look like hell, he thought, and then he looked around the room. And so does this house.

He began in the bedroom, gathering up the laundry and hauling it to a Laundromat. He cleaned the bathroom, the kitchen, the hallways, the living room, and the back porch. He vacuumed and washed and dusted and wiped and exerted more physical energy than he had in a year. After five sweat-soaked hours, he took a cold can of beer from the refrigerator, literally hauled himself up the long stairway, using the wrought-iron banister as a combination crutch and resting place. When he reached the top of the stairway, he opened the door to the small room that had once been his office at home. He hadn't actually worked in the room in five years, and he probably hadn't even entered the room in the past year. When he walked in, the first thing he noticed was the musty odor that dominated the entire area. Then he saw the great masses of mildew that covered huge cartons of books and papers and old magazines. A shield of dust had settled over an old, gray Olympia typewriter that perched on the edge of an ancient wooden desk which, even at that moment, was serving as an enormous repast for an army of insatiable termites. Adam coughed as the mixture of mildew and dust drifted into his lungs. He sipped the beer and felt its cool bite cut the tickle in his throat. He looked around the room at the remnants of his life. Old ad campaigns. A play that never got past the first intermission. Even old term papers and college yearbooks. He opened one dated 1952 and began to search for a picture of the young man he once was. But before he could find one, a white, typewritten sheet of paper, yellowing slightly at the edges, fell from the book and glided to a peaceful landing on a field of dust at Adam's feet. He picked it up and recognized it immediately. Incredible how the events of twenty-odd years that separated the eager boy from the tired man could disappear instantly, and he could see himself, alone in another room, composing a poem that summarized all the fury and passion and disenchantment of a sophomore mind alone in a godless universe. He read the poem slowly, his lips moving softly in remembered cadence:

Oh, man, oh, man, you are so vain
The wind, the sun, the moon, the rain
are not as you would have them be
elements to prove your majesty
for when your fickle span is through
the wind shall blow the rain on you
The moon, the sun, shall forget you soon
A futile chord in the eternal tune.

Adam folded the piece of paper and placed it back in the book which he returned to its dusty shelf. He noticed, under the desk, a small stack of photo albums. He immediately recognized the one on top, although he had not looked at it in years. It was his and Louise's wedding album. He picked it up, blew dust off the cover, then began to leaf slowly through the pages.

There was Louise in her wedding gown, frozen forever in the total radiance captured by the single click of a camera some twenty years earlier. There were shots of him and Louise waving from the back window of a limousine. Louise cutting the cake. Louise laughing as she tried to feed the first piece of cake to Adam, and had it slip through her fingers to land on his jacket. Funny, he could remember that as if it happened only a week ago. It had been a cold, nasty late November day in New York. He could remember listening to the Army-Navy football game while getting dressed for the wedding and hearing his best man, Dom Petrella, begging him to "get moving before everyone thinks you got cold feet."

Ah, yes. There was a picture of Dom Petrella holding a glass of champagne and smiling broadly at a girl who had gone to school with Louise. What was her name? What did it matter? Interesting how young he and Dom both looked. And, of course, Louise, too. But then he always thought of Louise as young. Even now. He tried to imagine what she looked like now. He hadn't seen her in what was it—twelve, fourteen years? At least. But then, Louise was as good as dead. And that reminded him of something his mother had said to him when he was a boy, coming from the wake of a young cousin who had died in a car accident two weeks before her graduation from high school: "She'll never change now. That's the way she'll always be in our minds as long as any one of us is alive. If you think of her thirty or forty years from now, Adam, you'll be well on your way to becoming an old man, but she'll still be a child."

Adam turned to the last page in the book. He knew what he would find there. It was a picture of himself and Louise, no longer in their wedding clothes, but dressed casually, and surrounded by suitcases and ready to leave on their honeymoon. They were eager to start their lives together.

Adam closed the album and reached under the desk to place it on top of the small stack when he saw the blue cover of the photo album that had lain beneath the wedding album. There was no dust on the blue cover. Adam did not recognize the album. He bent forward at the waist from his seat at the desk and reached farther under the desk until his hand touched the blue album cover. Then he pulled his hand back and placed the album on the desk in front of him. Across the front of the blue album cover in white block lettering were two words: "OUR SON."

He was certain he had never seen it before. But how did it get into the house?

Adam opened the album. On the first page was a cartoonlike drawing of a teddy bear. Beneath it was the printed phrase, "My name is," and beneath that, printed by hand, were the words Robert Reynolds. At the bottom of the page, there was a red rubber ball with green stars scattered over its surface. Between the stars were the hand-printed words, "My mom's name is Louise. My dad's name is Adam."

Adam turned the page. There was a close-up photo of a newborn infant, light hair, eyes barely open, tongue peeking between lips, ears close to head, puffed cheeks. And, of course, the harelip.

A printed form, followed by handwritten words, completed the page. It read:

My name is: Robert Daniel Reynolds
I was born: December 25, 1957
To: Louise and Adam Reynolds
Weight.......... Length..........
My doctor was: ....
Hospital..........
City.......... State..........

Adam studied the photo and again read the line: "I was born: December 25, 1957. He turned a page.

The baby was wrapped in blankets, his tiny head poking out from a sea of white. His hair seemed slightly darker, the features more rounded. There was a pacifier in his mouth, but because of the angle of the baby's head and the poor lighting in the photo, Adam could not see if the harelip was there. There were four snapshots, but the poses varied only slightly. Across the top of the page was printed, HERE ARE SOME OF MY VERY FIRST PHOTOS. Underneath this, printed by hand, were the words: "3 weeks, 1st day of Pablum."

The following pages were filled with photos of bassinets and toy monkeys and a baby that seemed to be forever sleeping and yet growing perceptibly larger from picture to picture. And there were periodic, handwritten notations.

"Getting bath." "8 weeks, 14 pounds." "5 months, 24 pounds." "Sitting up." "2 teeth." "1st birthday." In all of the photos, only the baby and some incidental articles were present. There were, Adam realized, no other people in any of the pictures. None.

As Adam moved through the book, the infant began to mature before his eyes. On one page he'd be crawling. On the next, walking. On the next, riding a tricycle. And by the time Adam had reached the middle of the book, the infant had become a boy celebrating his seventh birthday by blowing out the candles on a cake, the action of

pursing his lips to blow accenting the deformity of
his upper lip. Still, Adam realized, there were no
other people in the pictures. Only the boy.

Occasionally, now, as the boy kept growing before Adam's eyes, there was a color photo of him
climbing a tree or running, or posing next to a lion
in a cage at the zoo. And then there was a color
photo of him dressed in a blue suit and tie. The
handprinted notations along the sides of the photos had stopped, but this one looked as if it could
be a picture taken about the time of graduation
from grammar school. He was, Adam felt certain,
the same boy in the photo he had found in Roger
Martin's office the day Martin had died. The boy
looked about twelve, perhaps thirteen years of
age. The previous color photos had shown that his
hair was reddish-brown, but this one showed his
eyes more clearly than any of the others. They
were deep blue, alert. He was a handsome child.
Except for that lip.

Adam continued turning the pages, barely conscious that he was nearing the end. There was a
shot of the boy—about the age of sixteen—that
bothered Adam more than all the others because
something about it seemed so familiar. Was it the
look on the boy's face? His posture? Did he re-
mind Adam of Harold? Or Louise? Or even of
himself?

On the next page, there were four photos of the
boy—by now about eighteen, Adam guessed—that
showed him in a variety of locations and in different clothes. And yet in each one, the boy's upper

lip was bandaged, although in the first two photos
the bandages were large white patches, while in
the final two photos he was wearing little more
than a Band-Aid just above his lip.

Adam turned the page and found only a
white, empty space. He continued through the few
remaining pages, finding nothing, until he
reached the back of the book. There, inserted in a
celluloid sleeve on the very last page, was an article that had been clipped from the *San Francisco
Chronicle*. It was dated August 30, 1975. The
headline read: "California couple confesses to
raising aborted child." Adam began to read the
type beneath the headline.

"An unidentified doctor and nurse from San
Mateo, California, today told state medical authorities investigating the effects of experimental
research on aborted fetuses that they saved a 4 1/2
month old fetus from abortion more than 12
years ago and have been raising the child as their
own ever since." Adam did some mental arithme-
tic. The article had been written in 1975. And the
boy described in the article had been born twelve
years earlier. That would have been 1963. So the
boy couldn't be Robert.

Adam returned to the article. "The couple, married for more than thirty years, claim that the 'rescue' took place spontaneously during the perform-
ance of what was to have been a therapeutic
abortion performed on a woman who had contracted rubella (German measles) during her
pregnancy. The doctor, reported to have made

significant contributions to the field of gynecology over the past two decades, stated that he actually made the decision to keep the fetus alive during the course of the operation more out of a sense of scientific curiosity than any compassion for the fetus. Because he had sufficient medical apparatus at his home, the doctor said he was able to bring the fetus home and keep it alive there. The doctor, now retired, said he had remained silent for many years because to do otherwise would have been 'professional suicide.' Now victim of a usually terminal disease, the doctor says he has very little to lose and therefore no longer has a reason to hide the truth.

"His wife, the nurse who assisted him at the operation, said they were influenced in their decision to come forward by the fact that the natural parents of the fetus had recently died, and thus could not be hurt by any revelation. The doctor and nurse (husband and wife) team went on to say that they have told the boy—whom they now consider their son—the facts of the case, and that the boy has come to accept it fully. The most interesting fact of the entire episode, said the doctor, was that he realized that he had behaved like something of a Dr. Frankenstein in trying to sustain life not for any humane or moral reasons but simply out of curiosity.

"Nevertheless, he went on, that fetus (now a 12-year-old boy, slightly lame in one leg as the result of a birth defect) had grown to become the most important person in his and his wife's lives.

When testifying before the medical authorities, the wife was asked whether or not she and her husband had feared prosecution over the years on the grounds of betraying a patient's trust. She answered by saying that both she and her husband were well aware, during the years that the natural parents remained alive, that they might, indeed, be subject to suit on a number of grounds. 'But now,' she concluded, 'the only thing we could be convicted of is saving a human being's life. And I don't think we've reached the point where that is necessarily considered a crime.'

"The medical panel questioning the doctor and his wife declined comment, but noted that their opinions will be expressed in a written report to the American Medical Association later this year. The doctor, when asked if he believed him and his wife to be the only people in the world who had saved and raised a fetus scheduled for abortion, answered that he didn't think so. 'First,' he said, 'because it's a big world out there and the same impulse that hit me has probably hit others. But more than that: I think the maternal instinct may have taken over in some cases where only women doctors or nurses or even local women friends assisted at abortions. They may not have needed the medical apparatus that I had available to me. The life-force is a tremendous thing. It is astounding under what conditions it can survive."

Adam closed the album, his hands resting softly on the cover. He sat staring at the swollen veins that rose beneath the surface of his skin on the backs of his hands and wondered what they were doing there. He wondered why they were colored blue when the blood inside them was red. And he wondered what time that night Robert would be coming to visit him.

CHAPTER 13

Adam Reynolds lay awake, his eyes studying the surrounding darkness as if he expected something to materialize from the misty shadows of his bedroom. The luminous hands of the electric alarm clock on his night table confirmed his suspicion that he had been in bed a full two hours without being any closer to sleep than he'd been when he first turned out the lights. If anything, he was more awake, more alert. His senses, he was aware, were stimulated far beyond their capacity. It was as if some consciousness-elevating drug had been injected into his system and he could suddenly see and feel more deeply into his own being than he had ever been able to before. He smiled nervously in the darkness, and remembered what Dom had said about Harold stealing drugs. Perhaps he, Adam, had somehow been drugged. Or perhaps he was simply high on fear.

Adam Reynolds closed his eyes, and in his mind he could see exactly how the universe worked. He could see a single virus dividing and multiplying itself into millions upon millions of genes and then into billions, even trillions, of cells, and swirling and mingling and forming into precise patterns. And then he was entering into his own brain where he walked down an endless corridor of neurons and synapses and plunged into a swollen sea of flickering electrochemical charges that pulsed all about him in a constant bombardment of vibrating colors. And the colors were a hundred times more brilliant and beautiful than any he had ever seen. Even more exciting: he could hear the colors, each having its own unique musical sound, each blending with all the others to create a harmony beyond anything ever produced by men and musical instruments. The colors blended and dissolved into each other, creating kaleidoscopes which, in turn, merged into one magnificent crescendo and then disappeared into silence. Everything was still, quiet, the silence beyond eternity. And then Adam heard something move downstairs.

He opened his eyes and stared again at the blackness around him. What was that noise? The wind? A car outside the house? His imagination? He looked at the glowing hands of the alarm clock and was amazed to see that he had slept three hours. It was now nearly 4:00 A.M. There. There was that noise again. What was it? A door creaking? A cat scratching at the screen door? A tree branch brushing a window? No. It was none of these. Adam had lived in the house for so many years he knew every night sound it could make. He did not recognize these sounds, or even exactly where they came from. There. There it was again.

Was it closer than before? Adam sat up in bed and bent his head toward the door, as if being even a few inches closer to the source of the sound might help him determine what it was. But he knew what it was.

It was Robert or the ghost of Robert, whoever Robert was. Adam became aware, oddly enough, that he had to urinate. And he could not tell if he felt a greater sense of fear or curiosity. Beyond the bedroom door, a few feet from where he lay in darkness, an uninvited presence had invaded his house. There. There was the noise again. This time it was closer. It was on the steps. The sense of wanting to know who or what was on the other side of the door disappeared. It was quickly replaced by a paralyzing panic.

The noise was closer still, coming at intervals of ten or fifteen seconds. Adam wanted desperately to move, but could not. He pressed forward with all the strength and fury he could muster, and still he did not move an inch. An invisible wall kept him a prisoner in his own bed. Then he heard the noise again—now it seemed to be coming from right outside his door. The invisible wall suddenly collapsed and Adam was out of bed reaching for the phone before he realized he was standing. His hand trembled violently as he tried to lift the receiver quietly from the cradle. His eyes strained to see the dial. He would call the operator and she would call the police. There, the receiver was off the cradle. Adam placed it next to his ear and there was a full five seconds of silence before he realized that he'd had the phone disconnected earlier in the day.

Adam placed the receiver quietly back on the cradle and sat down softly on the side of the bed. He sat staring at the thin sliver of light from the hall that squeezed into his bedroom under the door, and he almost smiled as he realized how many times he'd seen this same scenario in films. The pursued, cut off from the outside world, cowering in a corner of his bedroom. The pursuer, slowly, methodically, stalking his prey. Sometimes there was a last-minute rescue. Sometimes there were violent murders. But that was in the movies. This was real life. Or was it? And what was real life?

The narrow border of light that had slipped into Adam Reynolds's bedroom, beneath his door, now disappeared. Someone had turned out the lights in the hallway. Or someone was standing outside the door, his body blocking the light. The bedroom now was virtually dark. Adam started to reach for the light switch above his bed when he heard the handle of the bedroom door turn slowly, painfully. His hand froze in midair and he surprised himself by screaming into the blackness of the bedroom, "Come on in, you cocksucker. What's taking you so long? Come on in so I can blow your fuckin' head off." He was amazed at himself for yelling what he had. How could he blow anyone's head off! With what? But maybe it might frighten away whoever was out there. And then Adam remembered the scissors in the drawer of the night table. He reached for the drawer in the darkness, banging his knuckles against the handle as he did so. Then his hand was inside the drawer and he found the scissors immediately. He withdrew the scissors from the drawer and placed them under the top bed sheet, his grip tightening on them until he felt he might squeeze them in half. "C'mon, you son of a bitch, bastard Robert or whoever you are. What the fuck are you waiting for!"

Adam again heard the door handle turn slightly, then stop. There was silence for five or ten seconds, and then the thin strip of light reappeared at the foot of the door and again slid into the bedroom. He's going away, thought Adam. Whoever it is, is going away. Adam relaxed his grip on the scissors and pulled his hand from beneath the bed sheet to soothe the bruise on his knuckles with his other hand.

Then, in the space of an instant, the light at the bottom of the door disappeared, the door was quickly flung open, and a searing white beam of light burned into Adam's eyes.

"Hello, Father."

The voice was a whisper of pain knifing into Adam's ears at the same time the beam of light blinded him, etching its frozen fire into his brain.

Adam lifted an arm to protect his eyes and instinctively curled his body into a tight little ball, in a feeble and, he knew, futile form of self-defense. He could smell something sweet and strange all around him. The smell of powder. Talcum. The smell of a baby's room. Adam waited for the voice to speak. There was only silence. Beneath him, Adam could feel the bed dissolving into a sea of quicksand, sucking his strength and his spirit. His legs started to twitch spasmodically, uncontrollably. The urine came in a rush, soaking him in a mixture of fear and shame. Adam shivered in the awesome silence, his arm still shielding his eyes, his body still contracted in a primitive position that prehistoric man might have assumed when he was savagely attacked by beasts far more powerful than himself, and sought only to protect his vital areas from merciless attack.

Adam tried to speak, but could not. The sounds that came from his mouth were not words; they were mournful whimpers. After a moment, he managed to stop his body from shaking. He found his voice. It was weak, frightened. But the words could be understood.

"Who are you? Why are you doing this to me?"

There was another agonizing silence, and Adam bit so deeply into his own lip that the taste of blood trickled across his tongue.

"Hello, Father."

The voice came to Adam from across the room and from across eternity. The pronunciation of the words was clear and distinct, yet the sounds carried with them an echo, an emptiness, that Adam had never heard before. It was not quite human.

A sudden eruption of sound underscored the stillness in the room. It was, Adam realized, the rattle of his bedroom air conditioner, straining past its capabilities to spill cool air into the Florida night. It was a sound Adam had heard a thousand times before, an everyday sound he had lived with for years. And yet it seemed the strangest sound he had ever heard in his life. The sound subsided quickly, and again the room returned to silence. The awful silence.

When Adam spoke, he again tasted the sweetness of his own blood in his mouth. "Are you my son? Are you my son Robert?"

Slowly Adam lowered his arm and opened his eyes. He tried to stare into the light, but it was no use. He spoke to the overpowering presence of the single powerful beam of pure light.

"I never meant to hurt you. I never wanted to hurt anyone. I just wanted to protect Louise. And myself. I didn't think of it as killing you."

There was only silence.

Adam's eyes were adjusting to the flaming glare of the light. Behind it, he could make out the silhouette of a human form. It was slight, a thin streak of black set against a deeper blackness. The light seemed to be held in the place where the intruder's face should be. It was as if the light were coming from his eyes. Adam could not see a single facial characteristic. Only the light. And the light kept staring at him.

Adam's voice was frightened, but stronger than before. "You cannot say I killed you. I did not kill you. I did not even want to hurt you. A doctor performed an operation. It's done every day. Thousands of times a day. And all the doctors said it was the right thing to do. What was I supposed

to do? Let Louise bring a deformed monster into
the world? You would have done the same thing
in my place. Anyone would."

As he spoke, almost without realizing he was
doing it, Adam had let his hand slip beneath the
sheet to seek out the scissors.

The light was a solid stream of silence locking
Adam's face in its gaze. Adam began to think he
could see strange fibers of a different kind of
light—blue vibrating streaks—spiraling around the
area behind the brilliant white beam. Adam spoke
again.

"Are you alive? Is that it? Did someone keep
you alive? I hope someone did. I swear to God, I
honestly hope someone did. Even if you're trying
to get revenge on me now, I hope someone kept
you alive. If I had it to do over, I'd keep you alive.
I would. I was too young then. I didn't know what
I was doing. The pressure. The pressure then was
awful for a young man to take. My career was just
getting started."

Adam was sitting up in bed now, staring into
the light, his voice pleading for understanding.
His hand found the scissors beneath the sheet.

"The doctors, most of the doctors said we
should do it. And Louise. Louise. No matter what
anyone says, the final decision belonged to
Louise. If anyone tried to have you killed, it was
her, not me. But you're not dead, anyway, are
you? All those phone calls. And the postcards.
And now this. You're not dead, are you? You
never died. You're not dead, I know it. You're just

doing this for revenge. You're getting even, aren't you? But you're not dead. So please, please, leave me alone."

The beam of light began to move slowly toward Adam.

"For God's sake, please leave me alone. Don't hurt me."

Again Adam raised an arm to block out the menacing light. Again his body hardened into a tight little ball. Again his hand squeezed the scissors.

The light was closer now. Adam buried his head in his hands.

Adam's body was frozen in a fear that transcended concern for his physical survival. It was the fear a man knows when he stands on the razor's edge between sanity and that one long irreversible leap down into the final, eternal prison of his own mind, the black pit of his own madness. Adam was ready to make that leap. Then he heard the door close. He looked up. The beam of light was gone. And whoever or whatever had been behind it was gone. But Adam knew it would be back. He screamed.

CHAPTER 14

Morning came like yellow fog, sliding through parted black drapes and rolling slowly and hotly into Adam Reynolds's wide-open eyes. He lay naked on the bed, motionless, the cool, muted hum of the air conditioner a faraway song his mind tried to hang on to. He moved his left foot until it touched his right foot, then moved the big toe of his left foot slowly back and forth across the instep of his right foot. He was not conscious of this action, but it felt good. It was soothing. After a moment or two he raised his right foot slightly and stared at the purple maze of varicose veins that sprawled across his ankle like the complex road maps of a city gone mad. His right hand moved to his chest, and swollen fingers brushed through a thick gray cluster of hair to find the sore that had been growing there for two full months. Or was it two years? What matter? The sore had grown larger, but less sensitive. A fingernail scraped across hardened scab and a soft, syrupy substance spilled out across Adam's chest.

Had Robert really been here, right here in this

very room only a few hours ago? Or was it a few days ago? And what did it matter? What did it matter if he really had a son named Robert or if someone was trying to drive him insane?

But who would possibly do that? Who could possibly hate him enough to go to such incredible extremes? Donald Schiff? Hardly. Dom? He was the only one who knew that Louise had been pregnant and lost a child. And Dom had always had an obvious feeling for children without parents.

Could that be it? Could Dom somehow have gotten things twisted in his mind over all these years? Was he seeking some kind of revenge? Revenge for what? Revenge for whom? Now that was something to think about, really think about, and try to remember. Didn't Dom say something years and years ago, about how Adam had better take good care of Louise. That's right. He had said it. He had said it a number of times. Now it was coming back. It was all coming back. Dom saying that Adam didn't know how lucky he was, and how he'd give anything to have found a girl like Louise. And how he would never get married until he found a girl like Louise.

"And he never did get married. In all those years, he's never been married." The voice was Adam's speaking to the emptiness of the room. Adam tried hard, very hard, to sustain the thought, to take it deeper, but he couldn't hold it. The sun was bright in his eyes and all thoughts of Dom slipped away as he remembered the light from the night before, its hot whiteness blinding him and serving as a blazing mask that hid Robert's face from his sight. He began to move, to rise from his bed, to do something, go somewhere, anywhere. He had no idea where he was going to go. He simply knew that he wanted to be gone when Robert came back. But first Adam went back into the small room at the top of the stairs where he had found the photograph albums. Everything was as he had left it except the photograph album of Robert. It was gone.

After he had gotten dressed, Adam left the house and contacted the phone company to reinstall service. Sometime later, perhaps an hour or so, he found himself driving to Donald Schiff's apartment.

It was at the traffic light at the intersection of Douglas Road and South Dixie Highway that Adam first looked into the rearview mirror and saw the driver of the car directly behind him. Adam could not see him clearly enough to determine his exact features, but he could see that the driver was a young man perhaps twenty years old. He was wearing sunglasses, the type with one-way lenses that reflect the light but keep the wearer's eyes from being seen. He had red hair.

The light changed, but it took the honking of traffic to make Adam realize that his car was blocking the lane. He pulled out slowly, glancing each second at the rearview mirror to see if the young redheaded driver was continuing behind him. He was. The young man was driving a dirty

brown Vega station wagon. The left-front fender
was pushed in toward the headlight, the relic of a
possible minor accident. He stayed at a reason-
able distance behind Adam—three, perhaps four
car lengths. When Adam eased his foot on the accelerator, it was as if he were actually driving the
Vega in his rearview mirror. He could see it slow
almost immediately, adjusting its speed to Adam's.
When Adam accelerated, the brown Vega picked
up speed, always staying in the same lane at a distance of three or four car lengths. As he drove past
the entrance to Rickenbacker Causeway and Key
Biscayne, Adam flicked his right directional signal
on. He looked in the mirror but could see no cor-
responding sign from the brown Vega. Just up
ahead was the turn off for Pelican Bay Towers.
Adam moved to the inside right lane. The brown
Vega followed. Adam slowed his car, then made a
right turn onto the driveway that led directly to
the Pelican Bay Towers Apartments on the edge
of Biscayne Bay. He looked in the mirror. The
brown Vega was gone.

Donald Schiff's apartment had changed remarkably since Adam Reynolds had last visited
two years before. Gone were the mocking political
pop art paintings and the stark-white modern
furniture. The walls were now lined with huge
blown-up photos of various galaxies in the solar
system. A billion stars surrounded the two men as
Donald Schiff directed Adam to sit on the simple
bench that stood where Adam remembered once
sitting in an Eames chair, flanked by a curving

metallic lamp that had reminded him of a cross between an astronaut's space helmet and the global hair dryers found in beauty salons. Adam was aware that things in the room were somehow different than they'd been before, but he couldn't quite get his mind to focus on, or care about, what was different. It was of absolutely no importance. The question was, Why had he come here? Why did he want to see Donald Schiff? What did it matter?

"Why did you want to see me, Adam? Is it about work? Have you changed your mind about that leave of absence?"

Donald Schiff sat cross-legged on the floor, a soft gray caftan covering his body. He looked at Adam intently, but there was no accusation in his gaze. "And why today of all days? Christmas Eve. Don't you have last-minute Christmas shopping to catch up on? I'm glad Christmas falls on a weekend this year. I couldn't bear another Christmas office party."

A fresh bay breeze parted the flimsy gauze drapes that screened out the late-morning sun. Donald Schiff had turned off the air conditioning in his apartment more than a month ago. It had been "too artificial, too far removed from nature."

"Christmas? Is it really Christmas already?" Adam's voice conveyed a sense of resignation rather than surprise. He sighed.

"Where have you been, Adam? One doesn't go around forgetting Christmas. A birthday, yes. A holiday, perhaps. An anniversary, maybe. But

Christmas, never. Not in a culture like ours, anyway. If you can make that cash register ring louder because it's Christ's birthday, then make it ring. We are not dumb in this country, you know. Almighty God and the almighty dollar, we honor them both on the same day, in the same way."

Donald Schiff folded his hands and let them come to rest on the pouchlike space where the caftan spread out between his crossed legs.

"I think you were right about reincarnation." Adam's voice was an apologetic whisper.

"What?"

"I know it sounds strange coming from me, but you mustn't laugh. Someone who never lived is haunting me. Either that or I am going insane. Or being driven insane." Adam rubbed his hand across his open-necked shirt, unconsciously picking at the small scab that was growing on his chest.

Donald Schiff sat silent. He nodded.

Adam spoke again: "You're the only person I ever heard speak about people being reborn and things like that." Donald Schiff noted that Adam's body was trembling slightly.

"I thought you might be the one person I could speak to about what's been happening to me, who wouldn't laugh in my face or think me insane."

"I won't do either," said Donald Schiff. "I promise. But first, you must tell me what's been happening." Donald Schiff spoke slowly, softly. He was not going to ridicule Adam. He was genuinely interested in what had happened to Adam, or so Adam thought.

"It began with a phone call," Adam said, "a phone call from a baby."

It took Adam the better part of an hour to relate the events of the past few months to Donald Schiff. During that time, Donald Schiff neither spoke nor made any gesture. He sat silently, absorbing everything Adam said, as if he could somehow transfer himself inside Adam's consciousness.

When he had finished talking, Adam was certain he had not covered every detail. But he was certain that Donald Schiff had received his message, especially the part about the visit from Robert.

A fresh wind from the bay once again fluttered the drapes and moved through the room like a casual guest totally at ease with the surroundings. It brushed Adam's face. He felt a chill. Finally, Donald Schiff spoke.

"Strange, isn't it, Adam? All these years, I have been searching for something. And it was you—you and all the others—who were laughing at me. And now you ask me not to laugh at you. But how can I laugh? I believe that all these impossible things that you claim to have happened, have, indeed, happened. But perhaps not in the way in which you think."

Adam sat quietly on the plain bench, listening to every word Donald Schiff spoke. Could it be that this cultural dilettante would be the one person to understand him, to help him? The superior tone and pinched, nervous look that had characterized Donald Schiff for years were nowhere in evidence. He seemed relaxed, his features placid. Was he at peace with himself? Or was he merely playing a new role with which he would become bored in a matter of months?

"The last time we really spoke about anything important was at the office. I spoke to you about the wisdom of Yoga and the reality of reincarnation."

Adam Reynolds nodded.

"You did not believe me then, but no matter. Because now you really have no choice but to believe. Not necessarily in Yoga, or in reincarnation. But now you must believe that there is more to life than your five senses can show you. Have you ever heard of parapsychology, Adam? Do you know what it means?"

Adam's fingers again played across the open-necked front of his shirt and found the sore.

"I think I know what it means. But I know very little about it." Adam found it increasingly difficult to concentrate.

"Perhaps parapsychology isn't even the right word," Schiff spoke again, "but what you've been experiencing has to do with the unknown, the unexplained. It may have to do with extrasensory perception or mental telepathy. With things that science can't explain, but which nonetheless do occur. People used to laugh at anyone involved in those areas of study before, but no longer. Now there are respected scientists who say that there is a type of psychic awareness that may actually be a step forward in evolution. For example, they believe that before all men could see color, only a few men could see color. But now, because only a few people can see past the barriers of the material world and into the richer world of psychic energy, most people say that these few are madmen. We say that they are insane. But isn't it possible that they are really the first to experience a new phase of evolutionary progress? That they are pioneers? Perhaps one day, all living men will be able to communicate in ways we dare not dream of today. Perhaps one day our minds will be able to penetrate beyond our present boundaries and we will be able to communicate with our own blood cells. Or see in our mind's eye what is taking place in another country, another planet, another dimension beyond those of which we are now aware. No, I don't think you are crazy, Adam, any more than I am crazy. Who knows? Perhaps Robert is really communicating directly to you. Perhaps he never died. Or perhaps he's alive at another level we can't reach or understand."

The room was charged with a concentration of energy that Adam had never before encountered. It was as if he could reach out and touch it.

"I don't understand. Are you saying that Robert exists? Or that he doesn't exist?"

"I'm saying neither. I don't know everything there is to know about psychic awareness. But I believe, as we are sitting here, that a mystical body of energy, an intelligence, runs through the universe and inhabits every microcosm of space. I believe that a very few people have discovered access to it, either by accident or evolution. I am saying that life, as we know it, is only one form of this energy. And that this energy is eternal. It cannot be destroyed. It will always evolve into new forms of consciousness. Perhaps Robert is an expression of that evolution."

"Two hundred million elephants." Adam's voice interrupted the hypnotic flow of Donald Schiff's words.

"What's that?"

"I was just remembering something you said to me the last time we met. You said that in a universe where a teaspoon of anything weighs as much as two hundred million elephants, nothing can be strange."

Donald Schiff nodded. Adam spoke again: "Are you saying that Robert exists? But that he exists only in my mind?"

"I didn't say that. I said that perhaps Robert exists. And that if he does exist, your mind may be the only mind that has access to him."

"Or maybe I'm the only mind that he has access to?"

"I suppose you could say that, too."

When Adam spoke again, his voice had a hollow sound, as if a great distance separated his thoughts from his words.

"Do you think it's possible for an unborn thing

to be destroyed and then exist consciously on some other level?"

"Yes."

"Why?"

Donald Schiff shrugged his shoulders and smiled. "Because I don't know what is impossible."

Adam was finding it increasingly difficult to focus his mind on what he wanted to say. He kept seeing flashes of the young driver's face in a rearview mirror. The red hair, the silver-lensed glasses. He finally spoke: "I told you there's a chance that when Louise had her operation the baby was never aborted, never actually destroyed. It could have survived. And for all I know I could be haunted by a human being who's every bit as alive as you and me. A human being who's waiting for me right now."

"A human being who was and is your son." Donald Schiff's face wore no expression at all.

Adam looked across the few feet that separated him from the strange-looking little man with the large glasses seated on the floor. The man looked familiar. Adam knew him. But he couldn't quite think of his name. Schiff, that was it. Schiff. Donald Schiff. But why did people have names, anyway? It didn't make sense. The person sitting across from him wasn't really Donald Schiff. Donald Schiff was just some words. The person sitting across from him was simply the person sitting across from him. Now that made sense.

Once again, a breeze from the bay moved

through the stillness of the room. Adam could feel it unnaturally cold and sharp against his face. The person sitting across from Adam again shrugged his shoulders, the loose-fitting caftan stirring with his movement. "What does it matter?" he said.

A sudden shaft of sunlight turned the lenses of the man's glasses into spheres of solid silver. Adam wondered what the man would look like if he were not wearing glasses. What he would look like if he had red hair.

"There, there," said Adam, staring harder at the person sitting across from him, "you could look like Robert if you want to. Maybe you really are Robert, if you know what I mean." They both began to laugh. Adam Reynolds rose from the plain bench and started walking toward the person sitting across from him. The man stopped laughing. The room became very silent. The man wanted to move, but he couldn't. It was too late for him to move or speak or do anything but accept his fate and hope that he would experience better karma in future lives.

Adam lifted the struggling figure over the balcony railing, then released him as the man tried vainly to clutch Adam's arms, or the railing or anything that would keep him from falling the twenty-two stories.

The scream was high-pitched and hysterical, but seemed to grow weaker as Donald Schiff descended through space with accelerating speed.

When his head hit the pavement, there was a sound like the sudden crack of a rifle being fired at a distance. At least that's what it sounded like to Adam Reynolds, who was staring down from the balcony, wondering if now, finally, the phone calls would stop.

CHAPTER 15

As he pulled out of Pelican Bay Towers parking lot, Adam Reynolds glanced in the rearview mirror. There it was. The brown Vega station wagon, about thirty yards behind him. Adam couldn't see if the left-front fender was damaged. But he knew that it was.

Adam turned onto Dixie Highway, then, instead of heading toward Coral Gables and home, he moved into the lane that led directly to the entrance for I-95.

How could Robert be following him now? It wasn't possible. He had just taken care of him, hadn't he? And yet there it was. The dirty brown Vega, framed in Adam's rearview mirror, remaining so constant in relation to Adam's car as to seem stationary. Well, Adam wasn't going to let Robert follow him home. He'd lose the brown Vega station wagon in the fast-moving traffic of I-95.

Adam sighed, settled deeper into the driver's seat, and pushed down harder with his foot on the accelerator. Without thinking, without even being aware he was doing it, Adam turned on the radio. As his car moved up the ramp onto the expressway, Adam realized that the voices on the radio were talking to him.

"Since it's been legalized," said one voice, "a lot of heartbreak and shame and guilt have been thrown out the window. A lot of careers have been saved. A lot of good marriages have been saved. And a lot of bad marriages have been prevented. I've paid for three abortions in my life. And I'd pay for more."

Adam squinted as he looked into the mirror. There were a lot of cars behind him now in a number of lanes. He didn't see the brown Vega station wagon. But he felt certain it was there somewhere.

Another voice spoke to him. "I think it leads to a philosophical dead end. The question really is whether abortion is good for the parents, and whether it is good for society. Because these are the parties that have to make the decision. No one forces anyone to have an abortion. Society certainly doesn't. Society doesn't advocate abortion. It's just that it no longer condemns it."

Adam reached for the radio. Why are these people talking to me? he thought. I've never done anything to them. He pushed one of the radio buttons to get another station.

Adam looked at the mirror. There were now only three cars behind him. The last one was a brown Vega station wagon.

Another voice came from the radio.

"Once the female ovum and the male sperm are joined, something new, something that never was before, comes into existence. Is it human? Subhuman? Prehuman? I don't know. But I do know this. It is a living being."

Adam quickly pushed another button on the radio to get a different station. There was a second of static. The voice continued:

"And it is totally different and distinct from the body of its mother. Its tissues are different. Its chromosomes are different. It is living, and unless interfered with, will grow and develop for nine months within the mother. And perhaps for as long as ninety years after it leaves the mother's womb. But from the moment of conception, it exists in its own right."

Adam wanted to turn off the radio now, but he was too frightened to take his hands from the wheel. He realized that his concentration was diminishing. He was beginning to drift from lane to lane. And those people on the radio really weren't making much sense either. What were they doing on every station he tried? And everything they said sounded so familiar, as if Adam had heard it or read it somewhere before but he couldn't remember where or when.

Adam looked in the mirror. There was only one car behind him now. A dark dot that was beginning to edge closer. Adam looked ahead at the road. He saw the exit sign for Hollywood Beach. He hadn't been able to lose Robert on I-95, all the way from Miami to Hollywood. But he knew he could lose him on Hollywood Beach, especially at this time of year with all the vacationers crowding the beaches. He turned off at the Hollywood Beach exit. The dark dot disappeared from his mirror. In a few seconds it was back, at the top of the exit ramp, maybe seventy-five yards behind Adam's car.

Another voice came on the radio. "A young couple with a week-old infant goes down in a plane crash," it said. "The mother and father die instantly in the wreck. But the plane's radio has been left on and is still working. And someone with a receiver picks up the infant's cries. Before you know it the story of an infant lost and alone after a plane crash would be front-page news. Rescue parties would be formed. Thousands would volunteer to search mountains and forests."

Adam removed one trembling hand from the steering wheel and reached for the radio's on-off button. He pushed it violently. The light behind the radio dial panel went off. But still the voice continued:

"Hundreds of thousands of dollars might be spent in an effort to locate him. Other lives might be lost and still the search would go on."

"Shut up, shut up!" Adam screamed at the radio. He pushed the on-off button furiously, frantically, over and over again. And still the voice went on.

"In a sense, when we look frantically for that child, aren't we looking for ourselves? Aren't we saying that if I'm ever lost or alone or cut off from life, do everything you possibly can to save me? Don't abandon me. Don't leave me alone to die."

Adam was seized with an impulse to stop the car and beat the radio into silence with his fists. But he knew if he stopped, the brown Vega station wagon could catch him before he reached the beach. And he knew that once he reached the beach, he could disappear into the crowds and be safe.

Again he reached for the radio. He pushed the on-off button. Then there was a soft little click as if a switch had been turned somewhere, and the inside of the car was suddenly silent, except for Adam's strained breathing. His hands tightened on the steering wheel as he drove down Hollywood Boulevard, its stores crammed with last-minute Christmas shoppers, its traffic moving in slow motion. Within minutes he would be on Hollywood Beach. One way or the other, he would be free of Robert.

CHAPTER 16

Adam knew a lot about the sun. He knew that
twenty thousand years ago, deep within a burning
mass of gases hundreds of thousands of miles from
Hollywood Beach, thermonuclear energy was
formed from the fusion of hydrogen and helium.
He knew that this thermonuclear energy produced
gamma radiation, which, if it had traveled directly
to earth, would have destroyed him and every living thing with which it came in contact. But instead, those deadly rays took some twenty thousand years to travel from deep within the sun's
interior to the sun's surface, by which time they
had changed primarily into the infrared and ultra-
violet radiations man needs to sustain life on
earth. Adam knew also that from the sun's surface,
these rays took another eight minutes to reach
Hollywood Beach, where they warmed his face
and shoulders and stomach and legs as he floated
alone in the water a hundred yards beyond the
long line of swimmers close to shore. In the
twenty thousand years and eight minutes it had
taken these rays to reach Adam Reynolds, they

had cooled from a temperature of 25 million degrees Fahrenheit to 76 degrees Fahrenheit. But Adam Reynolds now cared only that they were irritating his eyes, forcing him to raise a tired arm to shield them from piercing light, a light which made him think again of the dazzling beam that Robert had hidden behind. A cloud passed overhead, immediately cooling Adam Reynolds's face. He opened his eyes and stared up at the great gray mass that blocked out the warm yellow sun and now threatened to conquer completely the peaceful blue of the sky.

How long had he been in the water? Two, maybe three hours? Maybe longer? And what difference did it make? He was safe from Robert.

When Adam arrived at the beach, he'd quickly removed his shirt and shoes and socks, leaving them in the parked car. Dressed only in a pair of faded khaki slacks, he moved along the beach for perhaps a half hour, mingling with the people, disappearing into the mass of human flesh. He noticed that with most of their clothes removed, the people on the beach looked remarkably alike. He began to wonder why they were here, and what they were doing, and who they were. He knew what he was doing here. He was walking. And he knew why he was here. And then he remembered that a long, long time ago, Hollywood Beach had been the place where he and Louise would come on Saturdays and Sundays and whenever he had a day off. It took nearly an hour to drive to Hollywood Beach from Coral Gables, but Louise had always said the drive was worth it. She had liked the broad white sand beach and the little beer and hot-dog stands and the ice-cream parlor that you didn't have to cross the street to get to. Adam had liked Hollywood Beach, too. But he hadn't been there in a long time. He wondered if any of the people on the beach had been on the beach years before when he had been there with Louise. Maybe some of them would remember Louise. After all, it hadn't been that long. Only twenty years. Or was it twenty-five? The sand still looked the same. The water still looked the same. Why shouldn't the people be the same?

And then Adam began to wonder if the people on the beach had any existence apart from the beach. Did they have homes to go to? Families to join? Or were they simply people who existed on the beach and only on the beach? Maybe it's a mistake, thought Adam: all these years I've been thinking everyone had someplace to go. Maybe a lot of these people walking around are absolutely alone. Maybe they don't know another person on earth. Maybe they have no past or no future. They just exist here on the beach and they exist here only for me. When I'm not here, they're not here. Just like Robert. If I weren't here, Robert wouldn't be here. Maybe that's the only way I can get rid of Robert. If I'm not here, Robert won't be here.

After strolling on the beach for a half hour with no sign of Robert, Adam started to relax. And that's when he saw the young man in the bathing suit standing no more than fifty feet from him. The young man was slender. His hair was red and he wore silver-lensed sunglasses. He seemed to be looking for something, for someone. His head was turning left and right as he scanned the beach. He hadn't seen Adam yet.

Adam felt his stomach tighten and a stinging bead of perspiration drop into his eye. The young man's back was to him now. Adam resisted the impulse to run because he did not want to attract attention. He turned around and walked swiftly to the water's edge. He felt its wet chill on his toes and ankles and saw it stain the cuffs of his slacks. And then he walked into the water. A few swimmers stared at the tall man who was entering the water in his trousers, but after a moment the water was above his waist and no one noticed him anymore. Gentle waves moved against Adam's chest. He was aware of the scent of salt around him and then he slid beneath a small wave, letting it cover him completely. He swam gracefully underwater, but after a moment his lungs burned for air, and before he realized it he had surfaced at a point where the water was well over his head and where there wasn't another swimmer within thirty yards. He began to kick his feet slowly and move his arms in a way that took him farther from shore, all the while keeping his eyes on the people on the beach. There was no telling if Robert was still among them. And Adam Reynolds certainly wanted to be ready if Robert was nearby.

And so an hour or two passed, with Adam Reyn-

olds drifting farther and farther from shore, always keeping a constant vigil lest one of those
harmless little specks of flesh swimming in by the
shore or lying on the beach suddenly take him by
surprise. He remembered how surprised the man
sitting across from him in the apartment had
looked when Adam had picked him up and carried him to the open window. The man had struggled and kicked and fought with all his strength,
but of course he was so much smaller than Adam
that it was futile. Adam tried to remember why he
had done it, but he couldn't. And it had happened
such a long time ago, long before Adam had gone
swimming. What difference did it make? Certainly Adam couldn't be held responsible for
things that happened so long ago.

But now the cloud that screened the rays which
had been journeying to reach Adam Reynolds for
twenty thousand years and eight minutes grew
darker, more menacing. Within a matter of moments, other clouds, some of them nearly black,
rolled across the sky like an army of invaders des-
tined to meet in one violent battle. A cold, chilling
wind blew up out of the east. The water quickly
grew choppier, a line of whitecaps walked in endless array across the far horizon. Adam Reynolds
watched the hurried activity of people on the
beach, packing up blankets, folding chairs, dash-
ing about in search of children who had wandered
away. Thunder boomed in the distance and, with
its echoing force, plastic floats began to blow

across the sand like strange missiles from outer space. Beach umbrellas swayed in the wind. Swimmers moved toward shore and out of the water with a great sense of urgency. Another booming crackle of thunder was punctuated by the shriek of a lifeguard's whistle. And yet no one onshore seemed to notice that Adam Reynolds was treading water a few hundred yards from shore. A shivering streak of lightning exploded across the sky, and before he realized it Adam Reynolds was laughing as he rose on the cresting surf and felt the primitive strength and energy of the sea take control of his body. He could only see the beach at intervals now, between the rise and fall of the rapidly growing waves. And each time the beach appeared between waves, it was emptier and emptier, until finally he could see no one at all on the beach. Adam Reynolds knew the storm was only seconds away but he had no desire to come out of the water. He welcomed the pure power of nature, and if it wanted to destroy him, then he would be destroyed. The sky was so black now that it would have been difficult for anyone to believe it was still late afternoon. Adam felt the fury of the tide taking him still farther from shore, and then he felt it slow as the wind suddenly died and an eerie, peaceful presence seemed to make everything quiet for a moment. And then Adam saw him, about a hundred feet away, holding onto a small blue float. He was looking straight at Adam. Staring.

Adam could not make out the man's features at that distance, or even the color of his hair. But he knew that the man holding onto the float was being pushed closer to him each second by the tide. Soon he would be able to see if it was a young man or an old man, and if he had red hair. And then a great cylinder of wild, white electricity erupted across the sky, followed by a deafening burst of thunder and huge sheets of cold rain began hitting Adam on the head and splashing on the water about him. The wind roared again out of the east, more violent than before. The waves rose rapidly and the man holding onto the float disappeared behind them.

The rain continued to come like cold bullets strafing the sea. Adam Reynolds coughed up a stream of salt water that he had swallowed, just as the man on the float disappeared behind the waves. Adam was fighting the frenzy of the tide and trying to keep from swallowing more water. His arms began to feel extremely weary and the residue of salt water in his mouth and throat caused him to vomit suddenly. He coughed hard again, and began instinctively to make his way toward shore, the rolling sea and the sting of salt in his eyes making it difficult to determine the distance. A wave swelled toward the sky and then collapsed, carrying Adam with it, and before he realized how it had happened, he was only a few feet behind the man clinging to the small plastic float. The man's back was to Adam, his face and head half hidden on the float; only his shoulders and a small portion of the back of his head were visible to Adam. The man's hair was soaking wet, and through the almost solid sheets of rain pouring down over the sea, it was impossible to tell if it was black or brown or red.

Adam realized that the man on the float had followed him into the water to attack him unexpectedly, but instead the huge, rough waves had caused him to lose sight of Adam in the stormy sea. There was no doubt in Adam's mind that this was Robert. Adam began to swim as hard and as fast as he could toward the man who clung to the float. He was going to end it all now, once and forever, and the wild fear in his heart gave his body insane strength.

The sea surged at Adam's back and he could almost touch the feet of the person in front of him, and then there was sudden, startling contact as a wave carried Adam right onto the back of the man on the float. Adam felt his fingers plunge inside the man's mouth and touch his teeth and then slide out to slip across the man's eyes and nose. Adam could not be sure if it was he or the man who was screaming, but he felt the man's thin arms trying to push him away, to break free. But like Donald Schiff, the man was simply no match for Adam's size and strength.

They could not see each other as they struggled in the water, only feel each other's arms and bodies and desperation. Adam managed to get both hands on the man's shoulders and push him beneath the water. And then, with his hands, Adam guided the man's head and neck between his own legs where he seized the head in a scissorlike grip. The man below the surface pulled and twisted and then finally bit deep into Adam's thigh, tearing a chunk of flesh from the leg. But Adam felt no pain. It was nearly over. He squeezed and squeezed his legs together as hard as he could. He felt all movement from the man below the surface come to a stop. And still he squeezed even as he swallowed great mouthfuls of water and was certain that he, too, would drown, that he, too, would die. But it didn't matter. He was killing Robert.

He reached down with his hands and grabbed the man's hair with his hands. He pulled the head up to the surface so that he could see what Robert looked like, so that he could see if there was a strong resemblance between father and son. And then the man's face was next to Adam's, the eyes open and cold and dead. Adam stared at the face as he struggled to keep them both afloat. It was the face of a man about Adam's age, somewhere between forty and forty-five. "You're not Robert," whispered Adam into the wind. He held the man's head above the surface for about a minute, studying it intently and wondering how Robert had managed to fool him so completely. Finally he relaxed his grip, and the inert head slipped beneath the waves. When Adam reached shore, it had stopped raining. There was a stream of afternoon sunlight sliding through a crevice in the clouds. He heard a noise coming from the place where rays of sunshine that began twenty thousand years and eight minutes earlier poured through a crack in the sky. It was the sound of a plane descending through the clouds.

CHAPTER 17

The ice looked like a plateau of pure frozen air. The guard put one foot on it cautiously, holding his weight back at first, then letting it move forward. He pushed down hard with his foot. The ice held firm and solid as if it had been sitting there for a thousand years. The short, heavyset man in the black parka brought his other foot forward, and now his full weight was standing on the edge of the river. The back of a gloved hand brushed across his upper lip, taking with it a congealed chunk of mucus and what felt like a square inch of skin. He started to move forward slowly, his head slightly bent to protect his eyes from the piercing chill of a wind that was surely one of the winter's worst. As he moved out over the ice, the snow covering it grew from a thin powdery base to a three-inch white cushion. In some spots, off in the distance, he could see drifts that must measure as much as a foot or more. He was sorry, now, that he had decided to leave the group and wander off on his own. The afternoon light was losing its battle with the storm. He certainly did not want to get himself lost out here at this time of year. He heard sounds, winter sounds, but they weren't the sounds of Christmas. They were the brutal sounds of nature invaded by a visitor who wasn't wanted and who really didn't want to be there. His own breath came in harsh, heavy counterpoint to a wind that roared through the wool flaps that covered his ears and kept them warm enough for him to believe he might not lose them to frostbite. His booted feet crunched over the snow and ice. He heard something else besides the wind and the crunching of snow and the agony of his own breathing. It was coming from overhead. He looked up. A thin cigar of a jet was sliding across a gray canvas sky. He smiled to himself. It was the 2:10 United flight out of Buffalo, headed for Miami. What he wouldn't give to be able to afford to go to Florida for a couple of weeks to get away from this frozen wasteland. But unfortunately, security guards at state mental institutions didn't make that kind of money.

He was looking up at the United flight to Miami when the ice gave under his feet. His first conscious thought was that he didn't know where he was or why his legs and arms and face and body were on fire when they should have been freezing cold. The water covered him completely. His next thought, and he knew it was crazy, was that he had forgotten to wrap the Christmas presents, but that it wouldn't matter, because he would be dead in a few minutes anyway. And then his struggling, kicking feet felt the bottom of the river and he nearly screamed with joy because at least he knew he wouldn't drown all by himself on Christmas Eve. He might freeze to death, but he wouldn't drown.

After he had clawed and pulled and practically broken his fingers hauling his water-soaked body from the river, he sprawled out for a moment on the first really solid stretch of ice he felt would not collapse beneath him. He would just rest there a moment, he thought, and then he would head back to the group and the parked trucks. Oh, Jesus, Mary, and Joseph, would it feel good to get inside the van of the truck and turn the heater on and feel like a human being again. He was, he guessed, about a half hour's walk from where he'd left the group. A half hour, barring any further falls through the ice or other natural disasters; a half hour and then he would be safe and warm and he could let the others worry about finding the maniac who had slit Dr. Kiernam's throat. Why should he risk his life to chase down somebody like that, anyway? It was idiotic of him to try to cross that river in the first place. Suppose the maniac was on the other side? And suppose he caught up with the maniac and the maniac slit his throat, too? I'd be as dead as Dr. Kiernam, he thought. He wished he hadn't seen Dr. Kiernam lying there like that, his face on its side, lying in a sickening pool of blood and vomit: Dr. Kiernam's eyes not really eyes any longer, just two pure brown marbles that could not see or comprehend anything ever again. All intelligence gone. Everything gone. But now the hard ice against his face made him realize that he must get back on his feet soon or he might never get back on them again.

He used his glove-covered hands to push his body away from the ice, and in a moment he was back on his feet, moving slowly, carefully toward the black line of trees on the riverbank seventy yards away. The clouds were fast becoming a fury of blackness overhead. The wind was wild and sharp, cutting through his soaked clothes and stinging his body like dozens of tiny pellets fired from an invisible gun. The line where the woods began was closer now. Perhaps thirty yards. He would be there in a minute or two. And then, in another fifteen minutes, with any luck at all, he'd be back with the group and inside a heated truck. But there was still a distance to go and he had better be extremely careful. He certainly didn't want to fall through the ice again. But even more frightening than that: he didn't want to be attacked by a maniac leaping from a tree, or appearing suddenly from behind a snowdrift, frozen steel knife in hand, eyes staring wildly, insane laughter roaring through the wilderness. He had been through too much for that to happen. Dear God, don't let it happen, he prayed. Let me get home. Don't let that maniac be hiding in the woods waiting for me. Let her be anywhere else. She's had enough time to be far from here, miles from here. He looked up to the sky to pray to his God. Let her be far away, he said. Let her be on that plane to Miami.

And then, when he lowered his eyes from the sky, he focused them slowly on something in the snow some twenty feet directly in front of him. With the hard wind stinging his eyes, he could not tell if it was moving toward him or away from him. He could not, in fact, tell if it was moving at all, or even if it was alive or dead. Suddenly he wanted to turn and run. But instead he took two steps forward. And then he realized that, even in the freezing cold, he had entered hell.

CHAPTER 18

The barrel was cool and hard against his face. Adam Reynolds's hands slid along the stock, marveling at the smooth strength of mahogany. He pumped the lever, then spun rapidly and raised the .30–30 into position: butt firm into his shoulder, cheekbone buffered from the stock by his right thumb. His great-grandmother's face came quickly into focus on the peak of the sight at the end of the barrel. He inhaled deeply, then squeezed the trigger slowly, gently. If Adam Reynolds's great-grandmother hadn't been dead for sixty-five years, she certainly would have been dead at that moment. Instead, the tough-faced woman sat quietly on the bookshelf in Adam Reynolds's living room, immune to the damage of an invisible bullet fired by her great-grandson.

Next, Adam took aim at the Tiffany lamp that hung directly over the massive coffee table. Again he held his breath and squeezed the trigger ever so gently, his body a statue save for the slow, almost imperceptible movement of his index finger. In his mind's eye, Adam could see the Tiffany ex-

plode into a thousand fragments of Technicolor
and the globe beneath the lamp burst apart at the
same instant. He had power in his hands now: the
power of life and death. It was, he thought, nothing to be ashamed of. It was something that made
him feel proud.

Adam walked over to the coffee table and
opened the small cardboard carton resting on it.
Inside, in beautifully precise clips, were the clean,
metallic missiles. He removed a clip and loaded it
into the .30–30. His hands, he noticed, were strong
and confident, much steadier than they had been
in weeks, perhaps months.

Adam had decided to buy the .30–30 on the
way home from Hollywood Beach for a number of
reasons. First, the man on the blue plastic float
had not been Robert. And perhaps by now his
body had floated to shore. Second, he knew that
the death of Donald Schiff falling from his apartment at Pelican Bay Towers would create problems. The police would probably come around
asking questions. He should be prepared for them.
He should be prepared for anything. Third, on the
way home from Hollywood Beach, Adam had
done some good, clear, solid thinking, his first
really clear thinking in months. If the person in
the water wasn't Robert, then who was Robert,
and where was Robert? How did Robert manage
to get into Adam's house? How was he able to
know when Adam would be at home, and when he
was going to be away?

The answers were so simple and obvious that it

was amazing to Adam that he hadn't thought of them before. Harold was Robert. And Dom Petrella was Robert. They were both Robert. All this time, they had been working together to drive Adam insane. Adam laughed to himself that he could have been so stupid for so long. It was all coming to him now. The cats.

Adam's mind drifted back to the darkness of a night a million years ago. He was standing in the alcove, phone to his ear. Dom saying good night. The door opening and closing. Dom disappearing and, seconds later, a cat crashing through the living room window. A coincidence? And then the frogs and birds. And the photo album. It was so easy. Keys. Just like Harold had stolen the keys at Bay Hill. So, so easy. All Dom had to do was take Adam's keys for an hour or two, have a duplicate set made, and then return them before Adam knew they were missing. "It would have been so easy," said Adam, "because I trusted you, Dom."

This way Harold could enter and leave the house as he pleased. While Adam was at work. Or even having lunch with Dom. Or even when he was asleep in his own bed.

Adam felt a strange, sweet calm come over his body. Now that he understood, there was no reason to worry. Everything would work itself out fine. He would have to punish Harold and Dom for becoming Robert. He would have to punish them severely. But where was Harold? Had he really disappeared? Or was he hiding? Maybe he was even hiding in the house at this very moment.

Adam smiled again. "Come out, come out, wherever you are," he said. Then he laughed softly.

For just a moment Adam tried to remember why, underneath everything, he had always known that it was Dom. He knew it, really, from the very first phone call. Adam knew he had been close to the answer before, but somehow it had always drifted away. But now it had come back.

It was the way Dom had felt about Louise. A long time ago. When she was pregnant. Remember? Remember what he said then? Adam whispered the words: "You now have the two most important things any man can ever have, Adam: a woman who loves you and a child of your own. Don't let anything happen to them."

Dom had said those words over twenty years ago. Or was it yesterday? Adam shook his head in sadness. "My poor friend, Dom," he cried, "you're the madman."

Adam stood in the living room, thinking about his friend. Dom had been in love with Louise all these years. And he hated Adam because in his own sick mind he had blamed Adam for what had happened to Louise. Dom knew the pain that Louise had felt from losing her child. Her child? Maybe it was Dom's child, too. Adam had never thought of that before. Maybe Adam wasn't Robert's father. Maybe Dom was really Robert's father. Adam smiled again because he was thinking so clearly now. "But if I'm not Robert's father," he asked, "why is Robert after me? He should be after Dom."

Adam sat down in the large black Spanish chair. And now he began to feel himself becoming confused and frightened again. It was all slipping away. With great effort he forced his mind to hold still. Ah, yes. That was it. He had been thinking about how Dom and Harold were Robert. And how Dom had probably worked on Harold carefully and painfully over a long period of time.

Harold was told repeatedly that he was at Bay Hill because no one wanted him, that there were plenty of people in the world—people like Adam Reynolds—who could afford to give him a decent home, but wouldn't, simply because they didn't want him. He was told that Adam Reynolds was the same kind of man his father had been. And while Adam Reynolds hadn't murdered his wife, he had destroyed her life just as surely as if he had taken a knife and slit her throat, just as Harold's father had slit Harold's mother's throat before he'd slit his own. Well, Harold couldn't get even with his own father for what he'd done, but he could get even with Adam Reynolds. Mr. Petrella would help him do it. And so one night, they sat down together and worked out a plan to get revenge for Harold and his little brother and his mother and his dog and for someone named Louise and someone else named Robert. Harold was to do exactly what Mr. Petrella told him, and if he did, Mr. Petrella promised him that they would really get even with the "Mother Fucker."

Mr. Petrella said it as two words, "Mother
Fucker."

Harold had agreed to everything. And so the
two of them, Harold and Dom, became Robert. Or
so it seemed to Adam Reynolds as he sat in the
dusky silence of his living room, stroking the
length of the .30–30 as if it were a sensuous child.
That had been the third reason that Adam had
purchased the rifle on Christmas Eve, the realization that his friend Dom and that strange little
redheaded boy Harold were really Robert. And
that they would probably be coming to see him
that very night to help him celebrate the holidays.
But Adam also had a fourth reason for purchasing
the rifle, and, he thought, it might be the best reason of all. The fourth reason was really quite simple. It was Christmas. And no one had given
Adam any presents. Not one. So he had bought
himself the .30–30 and the carton of cartridges. It
was Adam's Christmas present to himself.

CHAPTER 19

The air on the back porch was warm and sweet with the scent of the semitropical plants scattered throughout the backyard. Occasionally, Adam could hear the strains of Christmas carols coming from radios in the neighborhood. His skin felt hot and sticky; the salt from the water at Hollywood Beach still clung to his body and hair.

He rose from his chair and moved to the carved Spanish bar at the corner of the porch. He selected a glass, then opened the small refrigerator set into the bar and removed a handful of small ice cubes from the freezer tray. He noticed that night had come to the back porch quickly, painting the entire screened-in room a mellow shade of blue. He deposited the ice cubes in the glass, then proceeded to pour in a large quantity of gin and just a drop of vermouth. Next he plopped in two olives and stirred the drink softly with the index finger of his right hand. Then he brought the finger to his lips, licked it gently like a cat washing its paw, and realized that the salt still on his finger from the water at Hollywood Beach interfered with the first taste of a martini that he'd had since that lunch with Dom. He lit a cigarette and let the smoke burn deep in his lungs before it slid slowly from his lips into the semidarkness of the back porch. He took a long, full swallow of the martini and nearly choked on its bitterness. It hadn't had time to chill properly. No matter. In a moment or two, it would be just the right temperature. He coughed and cleared his throat. A smile spread slowly across his face and he raised his martini in a silent toast to his good friend Dom. "Nobody lives forever," he said. "Not me. Not Dom. Not anyone." And then he sipped the martini slowly. It was colder and infinitely better than the first swallow. He brushed his free hand across the hardened scab buried beneath the mat of woolly gray hair on his chest.

Thirty minutes, four Marlboros, and three martinis later, Adam Reynolds realized that he would never be able to stay awake all night waiting for Robert or Dom and Harold to come to visit him, not if he kept drinking rapidly and didn't do something to ward off the fatigue which he now felt from the events of the day.

Coffee, he thought, coffee would do it. But first, a shower. Better yet, a dip in the pool. He opened the screen door and stepped out into the backyard. The air seemed a trifle cooler, a little less stifling than it had on the back porch. Above, the moon was a slice of neon. The stars were out. Millions of them. Adam heard a frog croak, then another. Then silence, which, except for the faint

strains of a Christmas carol, seemed to rise up out
of the black bushes that bordered the entire backyard. Adam tightened his grip around the empty
martini glass in his hand and then suddenly hurled
it like a grenade into the thick growth of bushes
behind the pool. A frog croaked. Adam laughed.
Then he quickly unbuttoned his pants and let
them fall to the ground. He stepped free of them
and walked slowly into the pool. He descended
the graded pool steps slowly, feeling the coolness
first around his ankles, then his knees, then his
thighs. He stood naked for a moment in the pool
before he realized he'd left the .30–30 on the back
porch by the Spanish bar. What's more, he remembered, he hadn't locked the front door. If
Robert should come in now, Adam thought, he
could shoot me with my own rifle. But he won't
be coming this early. Not on Christmas Eve. He'll
wait until a little later. Probably around midnight.

Adam Reynolds made the final step into the
pool, descending until the water swirled in cool
circles around his middle. The surface of the pool
was again covered with a great floating blanket
of green leaves and twigs which had fallen from
the giant poinsettia tree that dominated the backyard. Adam Reynolds brushed the leaves out of
his way as he waded deeper into the pool, wondering how a single tree could continuously shed
so many leaves. Millions upon millions, it seemed,
each year. And this was only one tree in one backyard. Think of all the millions upon millions of
trees across America. Not just the ones in the ci-

ties and suburbs, but the countless trees in the countryside, and the miles upon miles of forests. Think about the incredible growth in the Everglades. Trees seemingly growing on top of trees, gnarled, twisting mangroves sucking up water and sprouting life. And what about other places, other countries. What about all the trees in China? In Europe? In Russia? And what about the billions—surely there must be billions—in Africa, growing and shedding their leaves on the edge of deserts and deep in silent rain forests? And, of course, the Amazon. The awesome, monstrous, towering trees of the Amazon, blocking out the sun and feeding endless armies of giant ants. Adam had seen them once. Not in a film, but in real life. He had traveled by plane and then by boat to a small jungle lodge about thirty miles south of Iquitos in Peru. He had gone there to research an advertising campaign based on the most inaccessible and mysterious regions of South America. The unspoiled vastness of the Amazon, as seen from the sky, made Adam feel insignificant, the plane he had boarded in Lima, frightfully fragile. There were millions upon millions of trees down there as far as the eye could see in every direction. And this was only the Peruvian part of the Amazon jungle. What about Colombia and Brazil and the other countries its awesome, sprawling, surging life inhabited. How many trees could there possibly be? And how many leaves on each tree? And each of them alive and growing. More than billions. More than trillions. More than his mind could calculate.

Adam remembered, too, what it was like to sleep in the jungle lodge, a mosquito net covering a bunk only slightly softer than cement. Jungle scents everywhere. The air so thick and wet he could practically feel the trees and bushes around the lodge drinking in the moisture. And then, in the morning, off on an exploratory trail through dense underbrush and immense piles of decaying leaves and rotting foliage. Vines thicker than a man's torso. Pythons wrapping their massive power around unseen branches. Armies of ants ascending the tallest, widest trees he had ever seen, stripping the leaves clean in a ravenous feast that he knew was being repeated on a thousand, no, a million other trees in the Amazon at that very moment. The monotonous, unstoppable repetition and urgency of raw, naked nature, going on like this day after day, year after year, century after century, was more than his mind could tolerate. The ceaseless struggle of life to sustain itself, no matter where, no matter how.

And now, back in the civilized quiet of his own pool, he looked up at the great poinsettia silhouetted against the black sky, and wondered how long it had been growing. A hundred years? Perhaps. And he wondered how long it would continue to grow. And then he suddenly realized that he, like the tree, was quite alone. Twenty-five years ago he had left his parents' home in search of a freedom, a way of life they couldn't understand. He had walked away from traditions and people who had long since outlived their usefulness in the

world. And in all those years, he had never regret-
ted walking away. He had carved his own life out
of his own experiences, out of the pain and loneliness of losing Louise, out of the day-to-day conflict he found in his career. But now he was alone,
more truly alone than he had ever been before,
and quite afraid that he had gone mad.

Standing there in the pool with the water surrounding his shoulders and neck, Adam Reynolds
became fascinated by a circle of thoughts that
started with something Donald Schiff had said to
him a very long time ago. It was something about
how nothing could be strange in a universe where
a teaspoonful of anything weighs as much as two
hundred million elephants. He lowered his head
into the darkness of the water and swam to the
bottom of the pool. It was black down there. Totally black.

When he surfaced, Adam swam to the edge of
the pool, reached onto the stone patio surrounding
the pool, and felt around with his fingers for a
small plastic door. He found the tiny handle,
pulled open the little door, and flipped on the
light switch. Instantly the pool lights came on beneath the water, lighting the entire pool and cast-
ing a soft glow throughout the backyard. The light
filtered through the thousands of tiny leaves that
laced the surface of the pool, creating a floating
pattern. My Christmas decorations, thought
Adam. And then he looked up at the huge poinsettia and said aloud, "And you will be my Christmas
tree."

He cupped his hands and began moving them along the surface of the water, using them as traps to capture dozens of the lifeless leaves. He threw one handful of dead leaves after another out of the pool, but he realized that the skimmer basket on the side of the pool would be stuffed with leaves and twigs, blocking the flow of water back through the pump. He swam over to the skimmer and pulled open the top. With his right hand scooped like a shovel, he reached down into the skimmer basket, expecting to make contact with leaves and twigs all twisted tightly together. Instead, he felt something small and slimy. It slipped off his hand. Was it a bird's egg? A dead baby frog? He reached deeper into the skimmer basket and this time he had it. In fact, he had three or four of them. He could feel them sliding around in his hand.

When he removed his hand from the skimmer, he opened his clenched fist to see what he had collected. It was too dark, where he was standing, to see clearly, but they seemed to be baby frogs, probably killed by the chlorine and chemicals put into the water by the pool service company. He was about to heave them toward the bushes in back of the pool when he decided to take a better look. He waded over to a spot where the light coming from beneath the pool's surface was brightest. Again, he opened his hand. He held it as close to the light as he could and bent his head close to his outstretched hand so that he might see more clearly.

There were three of them, almost identical, perhaps twelve weeks old, their heads and arms and legs already formed, even their feet and fingers visible to Adam. Three tiny human fetuses.

He closed his hand as tightly as he could and squeezed until his fingernails drew blood from the edges of his palm. He opened his hand. A messy, syrupy pulp oozed across his palm and ran down between his fingers. It reminded him of the substance that sometimes poured out from his chest. He crashed his hand down hard into the water and began to wash it furiously, using his other hand to scrub it clean. And then in spite of the whimpering animal sounds that were coming from his mouth, he heard another sound coming from a million miles away, coming from the house. The phone was ringing.

He ran naked toward the house, not knowing why he was running, and then he was inside the screen door and standing on the porch, staring at the .30–30 propped against the Spanish bar. The phone was still ringing; it sounded to Adam Reynolds as if it were in pain. Adam Reynolds picked up the rifle and, carrying it at his side, walked slowly through the living room and into the foyer with its long hallway. Each shriek of the phone echoed across the emptiness of the house. Adam gripped the rifle tighter as if he were thinking of shooting whoever it was on the phone. And, of course, he knew who was going to be on the other end of the line. He lifted the receiver from its cradle and placed it softly against his ear and waited for the familiar voice.

"Hello, hello." It was a female. "This is long distance calling for a Mr. Adam Reynolds. Is he there, please?"

Adam stood mute, trying to understand what was being said to him, what was being asked of him. The female voice spoke again. "Are you there? Hello. Long distance calling for Mr. Adam Reynolds. Is he there, please?"

Adam smiled and wondered what was in store for him, what kind of a Christmas surprise Robert had planned. He spoke gently. "Yes, operator, this is Adam Reynolds."

There was a one- or two-second pause and then he heard the operator say, "Go ahead, please. Your party is there."

"Hello, Mr. Reynolds?" The voice was far away and unfamiliar.

"Yes."

"This is Dr. Gershreich. In New York. I'm afraid I have some bad news for you about your wife."

What wife? thought Adam. I don't have a wife. And then he remembered Louise. Of course. Louise was still his wife. "Go ahead," said Adam, his voice a whispering monotone.

"I'm sorry to have to tell you this on Christmas Eve, but I did think we should let you know as soon as possible."

"Yes."

"Your wife is dead, sir."

Adam knew he was supposed to say something, but he had no idea what it was. Finally, he forced his mind to focus on a single word and then spoke it softly:

"How?"

"Are you sure you want to go into the details right now, sir? I can put everything into a letter."

There was a knock on the huge pine front door. Adam glanced up at the door from where he was standing naked in the alcove, about twenty feet away. He ignored the knocking sound and spoke again into the receiver.

"How?"

The man on the other end of the line cleared his throat. "Unfortunately, sir, the events surrounding your wife's death were as tragic as the illness that brought her here in the first place."

Adam tried to concentrate on what the man was saying, but the knocking on the front door made it difficult.

"She escaped from her ward. No one knows how for sure. In any event we're virtually certain that she was responsible for the death of one of our staff members. A brilliant doctor. A personal friend of mine."

Again, there came a sound of knocking on the front door, this time heavier, more insistent. Again, Adam ignored the sound and continued listening to the person on the phone.

"In any event, your wife was found in the woods a few miles from here by a security guard for the institution. She had frozen to death."

The knocking had now become pounding, booming through the house and making it difficult for Adam Reynolds to keep his mind on what the man was saying. But he knew it was important. And he knew that it had to do not only with Louise, it had to do with Robert as well.

"She was found curled up in a ball like a baby in the womb, trying to keep warm. She was naked, except for some strange symbolic thing she had twisted into shape from a wire coat hanger. She had tied it around her body so that it protruded from between her legs. We think it was meant to look like male genitalia."

The banging on the front door suddenly stopped and Adam realized he should hang up the phone and go see who was at the door. But he held on for a moment longer.

"She had also clawed a name into the ice and frozen snow with her fingers. The pain must have been unbelievable because her fingers had been ripped raw."

Adam heard a wooden groan coming from the front door. He saw the handle turning and the door start to open slowly.

"The name was Robert, wasn't it?" said Adam before he quietly hung up the phone.

The door swung fully open now and two figures stood silhouetted against the dark night outside. They started to move forward, and Adam recognized the larger figure first. He could tell by the massive build. It was Dom. But who was that with him? Smaller. Slighter. And why were they walking toward him? Now the smaller figure was moving ahead of Dom. A beam of light from a streetlamp outside struck the figure's head. The hair was red.

Adam raised the .30–30 in front of his body with one hand. He pulled the trigger, and the explosion that roared through the darkened hallway ripped directly into the smaller figure's face, entering at the left side of the nose and moving diagonally through the right eye and out the right temple. The recoil of the weapon was so strong that the rifle nearly flew from Adam's hand. Before he could raise it again, he saw the other figure, the one he was certain was Dom, run through the front door and disappear into the darkness outside. No matter. He would be back. And Adam would be here, waiting. The important thing was that Robert had been destroyed. Adam walked over to the light switch. He wanted to see what Robert looked like, even with half his face gone. He turned on the lights.

Adam could not remember seeing the house look more beautiful. The Cuban tile floor became a sea of intricately interwoven and geometrically precise patterns that moved fluidly beneath his feet. The arches between the rooms were splendidly curving links that allowed him to move freely about, yet also heightened the sensation that he and the house were blending together, were becoming an entity, were becoming one.

He would have liked that, he thought. If he could literally become a part of the wall, if his being could penetrate the tile floors and the wrought-iron banisters and the pendulous chandelier. If he could lose the painful sense of his own physical presence and evaporate, so to speak, into the very essence of the house, then of course he would have an immortality of sorts. As long as the house stood, Adam Reynolds, in a sense, would be alive. But nobody lived forever. He knew that. He had always known that. And now he watched a river of blood curl across the Cuban tile floor as it flowed gently from a gaping hole in the side of the boy's head. Certainly, the boy would not live forever. Occasionally, his head quivered and his leg kicked, and Adam could actually smell death starting to breathe through the boy's lips, its sour stench filling the half-dark hallway. A bubble of blood appeared on the boy's lips and balanced itself there for a long moment before his next, almost imperceptible breath destroyed it.

They were gathering outside in the darkness now. Adam knew that, but there was nothing he could do about it. He had heard neighbors' cars starting up and driving away, obviously evacuating the area under police orders. He wondered if any police had reached the backyard. Or if they had taken refuge in houses across the street and decided to wait through the night, or at least until Adam fell asleep, before coming to get him. But he wasn't going to fall asleep. Someone had to keep an eye on the boy; someone should be present when he died. No one should ever die alone, thought Adam. It's just not right. Louise had died alone. And that wasn't right.

He could hear the boy's breathing. It had

grown strangely louder in the space of a few moments: frantic, convulsive gasps for oxygen, followed by a slow, long, wheezing hiss like the air being let out of a bicycle tire. Adam wondered for a moment if he shouldn't walk over to the boy and put another bullet through his brain and bring his suffering to a halt. But something made him decide not to. Adam knew that his own life would soon be coming to an end and the boy might be able to keep him company during his own final hours.

He did wish the boy could speak, though. There were so many questions he wanted to ask him. Who was he? And where had he really come from? Had that been Dom Petrella with him in the doorway? But that wasn't really a question. Adam knew it had been Dom. There was no mistaking that massive build, even in the darkness.

The desperate, gasping struggle for air came again, an unconscious quest for survival, for life. Only this time, the wheeze that followed was softer, weaker. Maybe five minutes left, thought Adam. Maybe ten.

Again, blind Nature, not knowing that the boy lying on the hallway floor was already past help, forced his lungs to play out the ritual of seeking oxygen to feed blood cells which were flowing into parts of his body that were already dead.

The phone rang, and the suddenness of its sound in the deathly still of the hallway caused Adam to pivot quickly and raise the rifle in readiness. By the time it rang again, he had already lowered the .30–30 and was walking rapidly to the alcove where he had answered that very first phone call from Robert so long, long ago.

He lifted the receiver and said nothing, waiting silently to hear Robert's voice.

"Adam, Adam. Is that you?" It was Dom. "Adam, oh, Adam. Why? Why did you do it?"

Adam answered softly, "Because of what you were doing to me. You see, I know now, Dom, that it was you. You and Harold. I know that you and Harold were making the phone calls and sending the postcards and killing those animals. It was you two, all this time. There is no Robert, is there, Dom? There never was a Robert, was there, Dom? You did it all for Louise, didn't you? And now Louise is dead. Did you know that, Dom? Louise is dead."

Dom's voice was calmer now. "Listen to what I have to say, Adam. Please listen very carefully. No one wants to hurt you. I never wanted to hurt you. I only brought Harold over to see you tonight to prove to you that he wasn't the one doing all those things you said were being done to you. He couldn't have been the one. Because he's been in jail in Deland for the past few months. He was in there practically the whole time since he ran away from Bay Hill. He was locked up four days after he ran away. He only got out yesterday. I know, because I went up to Deland to get him."

"I don't believe you."

"It doesn't matter what you believe, Adam. Not anymore." There was a short silence on the line. "Is Harold dead? Did you kill him?"

Adam looked over at the figure sprawled on the floor ten feet from where he stood in the arch of the alcove. The boy was still breathing. But it really didn't matter.

"Yes. He's dead. I killed him."

"Adam. Listen to me. I'm with the police. We're across the street. That's where I'm calling from. There are policemen all around your house right now. But please believe me, Adam. No one wants to hurt you."

Dom hesitated, waiting for some word, some sign that Adam understood what he was talking about. There was only silence.

"You were right about one thing, Adam. There is no Robert. There never has been. He's only existed in your mind. So please, Adam, don't let anyone else get hurt because of someone who doesn't even exist, who never existed. Please, Adam. Let us help you. Put down your rifle and walk out the front door. I swear no one will hurt you. If you don't, the police will have to come in after you. You can't keep them out forever."

Adam removed the phone from his ear and looked into the receiver. It was as if he were talking directly to the receiver instead of to Dom.

"I did get the phone calls, Dom. I did talk to Robert. I did see dead cats. I did touch dead birds and frogs and babies. I didn't do those things to myself. I didn't make them up. I didn't. I didn't."

There was a long pause, then Adam spoke again: "I cannot come out," Adam said, "I must stay here with my son. He is my son, you know."

Adam hung the receiver back in its cradle and walked slowly over to where the still figure lay sprawled on the Cuban tile floor. He knelt.

The boy's one remaining eye was open, but he could not see Adam, nor would he ever see anything again. The empty socket was filled with blood, flesh, splinters of bone, and mucus. It seemed to be staring at Adam. He touched the boy's forehead; he felt the boy's heart.

"Why did it come to this?" he said. "Why did you do this to me?" The boy did not answer. He did not breathe. He was dead.

Adam cradled the boy's head in his own tired hands. Instinctively, he began a slow, rocking motion. He held the boy's head to his chest, mindless of the blood and gristle that spilled onto his own body. And then Adam began to cry. He cried softly, but bitterly, that no one else was there to mourn his only son's death. He cried, and in his heart he cried, too, for every father who had ever lost a son, every mother who had ever lost a child, for everyone who had ever lost anyone. He cried for Louise and for Dom and for himself. He cried for everyone who had ever walked the earth. And then he cried for those who had never walked the earth and for those who never would. And that is when he cried the hardest.

And as he cried, he began to feel himself rising out of his body, as if his mind had suddenly been released to float free in space. From a distance, he could look down and see the man who was himself, cradling the dead boy and rocking gently back and forth. And he knew that soon his own pain, his own life, would cease, and that the trillion upon trillions of cells that had been Adam Reynolds would decay and disappear into dust, and then into the cosmos, until there would be no trace, no evidence that Adam Reynolds had ever existed. He would simply no longer be. In the endless cycle of eternity, he would be no larger or smaller than Robert. They would both be equal parts of the universe, their spirits inseparable. They would both be everywhere and nowhere, simultaneously and together, forever and ever. And then he understood, finally, that as soon as he was free of the physical being and tortured mind of Adam Reynolds, he would not merely be joining Robert, he would become Robert. And now he understood, too, that he and Robert had always been together and were only separated by the deceitful veils of time and space, and that soon they would be together always and always and always.

Adam Reynolds continued to cry through the long night, kneeling on the hard floor, holding the dead boy's head to his chest. At dawn, as the first gray light of Christmas morning moved through the old house and surrounded the man and the boy, Adam stopped crying. He kept rocking the boy's head on his chest and he began to sing. He sang a lullaby. It was "Brahms' Lullaby." He sang it softly and gently so as not to wake his son.

When they came through the front door, that is how they found him: kneeling on the floor, singing softly to the boy in his arms.

He was still singing when they took him through the front door and out into the sunshine. And he was still singing when they put him into the car.

Just before the door of the car closed, Adam heard the phone ringing inside his house. He tried to get back out of the car, but the handcuffs made it awkward for him to move, and a huge, strong hand grasped his shoulder firmly and held him in place. Adam looked up into the eyes of the man in the dark suit seated beside him in the car. The man's eyes were sympathetic. The man understood.

Inside the house, Dom Petrella picked up the phone and placed it next to his ear, turning as he did so to face the police captain who stood motionless in the hallway. Dom said nothing, but appeared to be listening so intently as to cause himself physical pain. His lips tightened. His eyes stared straight ahead at the police captain, but they did not see him. Dom Petrella's hand began to quiver slightly, his swarthy complexion seemed slowly to turn a soft gray in the morning light of the hallway.

"Who is it?" asked the police captain. Dom stood silent, his eyes blank, uncomprehending. The police captain stepped quickly toward the alcove, but before he could reach it, Dom had gently placed the phone back in its cradle on the wall. Then Dom Petrella spoke, but his voice was so low that it could not be heard clearly, even by the police captain who was now standing beside him.

After a moment's silence, Dom spoke again, not to the police captain or even to himself or to anyone except the emptiness of the old house.

"It was no one," said Dom. "It was no one at all."